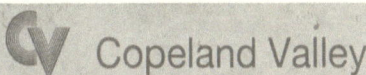

Copeland Valley

Your Cities,
Your Tombs

Jordan Krall

YOUR CITIES, YOUR TOMBS
Jordan Krall

Published by

Copeland Valley Press

Copelandvalley.com

Also by Jordan Krall

False Magic Kingdom

Bad Alchemy

The Gog and Magog Business

AUTHOR'S NOTE

This book is the last in a series. In order to understand the events depicted in this book, the reader
should first read FALSE MAGIC KINGDOM and
BAD ALCHEMY. They should also read THE GOG
AND MAGOG BUSINESS if possible.

Jordan Krall
September 11, 2012

"The people who have really made history are the martyrs."
-Aleister Crowley

Dedicated
to
my closest friends

"Don't wait for the Last Judgment. It happens every day."
-Albert Camus

B.C.

Three chariots appear on the horizon. You blink and they are gone. You blink again and they return. They are larger now and their shape has been slightly altered. They resemble automobiles and then they do not. They resemble airplanes and then they do not.

They are chariots again.

You are afraid to blink a third time so you use your fingers to keep your eyes open even though the desert sand is blowing in your face.

A giant humanoid figure appears behind the chariots and kneels down. You cannot make out many of the figure's features but you can make out an eye and that eye is looking at you. And still you do not blink. You just stare.

The chariots appear to move in place, spinning in a way that prevents you from getting a good look at them as you walk slowly in their direction. Your fingers are still holding your eyelids open. You will not blink.

The humanoid figure rises and now you see both of its eyes and they are looking at you. It steps over the chariots and is approaching. You just stare.

Your body wants to blink but your curiosity refuses to comply. The figure is walking towards you, getting closer, and the chariots fade into the horizon. You decide your body does not need any more stress so you let your eyes blink.

The figure is standing only a few feet away from you but now it is small compared to you. It is practically a doll. You return your fingers to your eyes and stare without blinking.

You will never blink again.

A.D.

Cars make a lot of noise and that's why you hate them.

They cause a lot of pollution, too. They are ugly, me-chanical insects scurrying around your beautiful city. You'd much rather walk. You expect everyone else to do the same. Is that unrealistic? Yes, but that doesn't stop you from having all of your absurd preferences. You demand everyone subscribe to your likes and dislikes.

As you walk down the street, muttering useless curses under your breath, you imagine all the cars bursting into flames. It is not an unholy thought, you decide, because you do not necessarily wish harm on the occupants but rather just the machines they operate. You'd much rather the people join you in your walk.

You reach your building. It is a beautiful building.

Buildings are beautiful in every shape and form, you think. You wish you were a giant so you could hug the buildings, kiss them, and explore them intimately. This is not a ridiculous thought. People build models, do they not? They stand around miniature train sets. They act out their fantasies of being giants.

You enter your building. It has a beautiful foyer. Everything about it is stunning.

You decide to take a walk around the foyer before you go to your floor where your friend will be waiting. You are early. You might as well make good use of the time.

You walk over to a painting you don't recognize. It doesn't belong here. That bothers you just a bit. No, it bothers you a lot. You don't like the change. No one has the right to change the beautiful foyer, *your* foyer. This is ridiculous.

You are now fighting the urge to tear the painting from the wall and destroy it.

You have never felt this much of a destructive urge before in your life. Even your fantasies about the flaming cars are nothing compared to this desire to obliterate the painting, this desecration of the foyer in your building.

But you do not destroy the painting. You *cannot* destroy the painting.

Instead, you walk out of the building and onto the sidewalk. You give your building one last look and then step out into traffic.

You will never return to your building again.

PART ONE:
Spears

I. AL JEEL SUNSHINE YEARS AGO

Barry stands in front of the mirror, nervous. In just a few minutes, he'll be a married man.

The door opens and a grey-haired man walks in, smiling and extending his hand. "Sorry I'm late. I'm Reverend Martin. Nice to meet you, Barry."

"Nice to meet you."

"Nervous?"

"Yeah."

"Well, you should be." The reverend laughs. "You'll be fine. This is a blessed moment in your life."

"Yeah, I know."

"I apologize for not coming here earlier to meet you."

"It's no problem."

"I wanted to give a quick introduction so you know a little bit about me before the ceremony. Just to give you a little background, I've been with Doylestown Trinity Church for twenty-three years. Before that I was a chaplain at Marburg Hospital and before *that* I was an astronaut."

"What?"

"Pardon?"

"What do you mean? Astronaut?"

"Before becoming ordained, I was an astronaut. In fact, that's what led me to my religious vocation."

"Okay." Barry is confused. His head is already spinning from pre-marital anxiety. The grey-haired man's astronautical confession has made it worse.

"You know, when a man goes up there, sees his planet from the point of view as *someone else*, as an observer, an outsider, it is natural to think about one's place in the universe. Then when you set foot on the moon, well, that's a whole new thing altogether. It's a life changing experience…much like marriage. So now we're back at square one, ground zero. Marriage. What a blessed event."

The man's words are barely registering in Barry's mind. He doesn't know if he is even hearing the man correctly. He needs a drink of water.

"Are you thirsty?" the reverend asks.

Barry nods. The reverend steps to a small table in the corner of the room. He comes back holding a water bottle which he hands to Barry.

"Thank you." Barry takes a drink.

"You're welcome, Barry. You're welcome." The reverend smiles, nods his head. "Do you have any questions?"

"No, I don't think so."

"No questions at all? About anything?"

"No…"

"Your wife had a lot of questions."

"Oh?"

"Yes. In fact, that's why I'm late. She had *a lot* of questions."

"What about?"

The reverend chuckles. "Oh, you know I can't tell you. She asked me those questions in confidence. All I can say is that she sure asked a lot of them."

Barry becomes feverish. "Should I be worried?"

"Oh, no, no, Barry, of course not. A nice man like you should *never* be worried. Everything will be fine, Barry. Now just relax."

"Okay."

"Take another drink and relax, Barry."

Barry listens to the reverend and takes another sip from the bottle.

"That's it, Barry, just relax. Now I'm going to get ready and I'll see you out there. You'll do fine."

Barry nods.

The reverend chuckles and leaves the room.

Barry faints.

II. HASHEM'S RAZOR

Sooner or later the firmament will crack from the momentum, the velocity, the sheer geometric horror that is public revelation, the shedding of the veil, the opening of the curtain.

This is broadcast number zero.

We know our competition. Our competition is the moon. Our competition is the poorly-maintained molecules of security. Our competition is mystery enclosed in a black box and buried in lunar rubble. In the box: voices lulling us into safety with explanations and supplications but we will use them as our own prayers and remnants of ancient charms. We will sit and listen, transcribe every word, file them away and then sleep, hoping for dreams of twin moons deflating into the limp eyes of god.

So there are crosses of wood stuck in the earth, crooked but sturdy, sturdy enough to hold our weight. We spend weeks studying our texts, memorizing the recordings and then finally: liftoff.

The soil, electron infused, glows and buzzes and we are taken away but our bilocation enables us to see the spectators on the ground as they go through their public rituals and our personal belongings. The rituals offend us in their simplicity. They do not respect our perimeters.

Sooner or later our own experiments overwhelm us and we are left blanketed in ash and poor excuses for human beings. Our very existence depends on this shaky theory and we will hold onto it through every earthquake and seizure that attacks us.

The chariots await our business. The chariots and faces and wheels await our proposal. Everything waits for our important decision. The firmament wrinkles up like an old face soured by an unfunny joke.

We get down to business. We get down to the root of the matter, the very core of things. We turn on the computers.

Soon we will be able to walk up those stairs or take those elevators to the roof of the moon without feeling like our grey matter is dissolving into cosmic dust.

Soon, we'll be whole again.

III. SOMETIMES RUMORS ARE TRUE

"If our patient wants it, then we'll do it," Dr. Sotos says to his two colleagues who are sitting in front of his desk. "The risk is high but the patient is providing us with a valuable service."

Dr. Visna shakes his head. "Just seems like a lot to go through. I think we can do much less and get similar results."

"We can't settle for less, Visna!" Dr. Corbelli says, slapping his palm on the desk.

"Easy for you to say. I'll be doing most of the post-op work."

"And? And? What's your point, Visna?"

Dr. Sotos pushes his chair back and says, "Gentlemen, please."

The other two men stop talking and watch as Sotos pulled a cigar box out of his desk. He opens it and digs around inside with two fingers. He says, "Our responsibility is not only to the patient, as you know. We are responsible to ourselves, our own consciences. If that means working a little more than we'd like, well, then so be it."

Dr. Visna nods. "Oh, I nearly forgot about my conscience!"

The doctors laugh.

Dr. Sotos takes a cassette out of the cigar box and puts it into a small cassette player. He presses PLAY.

The doctors spend the next hour looking over charts, medical books, x-rays, photographs, drawings, and their own notes while listening to the sounds of things, the cacophony of their years of practice, the echo of exploratory procedures, the noise of achievement.

Poor quality voices hiss from the speakers: "...but more often than not I pinch the skin between my thumb and index finger until the pain pushes me into blackness for I do not want to hear anything but my dry skin cracking. That is what brings me those dreams of hiding in an industrial park..."

Dr. Sotos throws three pills into his mouth and swallows them dry. He puts his right ear to the speaker and listens: "That's when I spotted the guy on the bicycle. He was watching the fiery building with the rest of the crowd but he kept looking back at Peter and me. The guy had a long neck and a face covered in birthmarks. He looked like a giraffe..."

Dr. Sotos presses STOP.

The windows behind his desk are rattling.

White plaster dust falls from the ceiling.

The doctors laugh.

IV. PAX OLLOPA

Ronald hasn't seen his wife in days.

Before he leaves for work, he checks on her but she doesn't answer him when he knocks on the basement door. He does the same after he comes home from work.

"Susan?"

She says, "There's a reason why I'm cutting it close."

Ronald knocks louder. "Cutting what close? Open the door, Susan."

"Yeah, I know the water is black."

"Susan! Who are you talking to? Open the goddamn door!"

"Yes, the rice is in the water, yes, I know."

"Susan! Who are you talking to?"

"Death squads!"

Ronald gives up trying to talk his wife out of the room. He kicks the door. He kicks it again. He forces his shoulder against it and gets the door open.

The basement walls are plastered with newspaper articles.

Still no answer from the ISS.

American prison labor means longer unemployment lines.

West scrutinized over ties to death squads.

Man, 23, fires gun at "moon".

Retired general sentenced for ritual killings.

Teenager, 16, accused of decapitating political official.

Ex-security chief to be sentenced for torture of controversial author.

There are threats everywhere.

Filmmaker murdered by extremist.

Helicopters.

Gluten.

Prions.

Lynching.

Sewage.

Pills.

Atoms.

Child molestation.

Kidnapping.

Suicides.

Blind combatants.

Detonating cords.

Implosions.

Public rape.

Hit squads.

Mail fraud.

Acid attacks.

Hate crimes.

Simple murder.

"Susan?" Ronald sees his wife sitting in front of a CB radio. She is wearing a black scarf that covers most of her head. She is turning knobs on the radio and whispering.

Ronald slowly walks forward. "Susan…"

His wife turns around.

"Which flight are you on?" Susan whispers. "And what seat are you in?"

V. PRINCIPLE OF A CITIZEN'S UTOPIA

Tina drinks the medicine.

What did Dr. Corbelli tell her? Oh yes, he said to drink the entire gallon in a half hour. It tastes like chalky bile. It tastes like this despite it being "cherry" flavored.

She decides she should have chosen the "grape" flavored one.

She drinks more of it.

Her stomach churns, bubbles, and she finds herself on the toilet, her bowels emptying. She wishes she had brought the television into the bathroom but it is too late now. Her bowels won't stop moving. She cannot leave the toilet.

Tina looks down at her penises. She is glad she is going through with the procedure. She is glad she was able to get enough money from her cousin to afford a motel room.

She realizes this, the day before surgery, is probably more stressful than the actual procedure.

Probably.

After all, as much as Dr. Corbelli explained what he'd be doing, Tina still didn't completely understand. Much of what he had told her was medical jargon. She trusts him, though. She has always trusted those who possessed more knowledge than she. Intelligent people are inherently *good* people.

Tina continues to drink the medicine. She finishes it. Her bowels continue to empty into the toilet. She becomes lightheaded.

The sink in front of her starts to warp, the faucet growing larger while the rest of it shrinks. Black water drips from the spout. The faucet grows and grows until it finally engulfs the entire wall.

Tina is now at the entrance to a subway.

Her bowels continue to move as she feels herself drift into the subway entrance and through a tunnel of orange light. There are people around. They're standing on both sides of her as she makes her way down.

She knows she's not dying. She knows dying wouldn't be this simple, this contrived.

It's the medicine, she thinks. Side effects may include dizziness, stomach cramps, dry mouth, fever, hallucinations…

The people around her are wearing white surgical masks. Their eyes are tearing. They wave at Tina. They are warning her about something.

Now she's at a subway station that's covered in dust.

"I don't want to be here," she says. "Side effect or not,

I don't want to be here."

Tina is not letting the medicine beat her. She needs to be brave and strong. She cannot let herself get down the day before surgery.

A voice from the dust says, "Never forget! You are invited to a supreme truth party! Happy!"

Tina is not shocked at the talking dust. She says, "No, I'm not."

"What flight were you on?"

"I wasn't on any…."

"You were on that flight, weren't you?"

"No!"

"You lurked on the threshold…"

"No!"

"Whoever invited you here must have made a mistake. Certainly you do not belong here…"

"I don't."

"What flight?"

Tina falls backwards and hits her head on the toilet.

The subway tunnel collapses.

The sink is normal now.

Tina falls off the toilet and onto the bathroom floor.

"I wasn't on any flight…."

VI. IS WHAT IT IS

There is no promise of any kind by the company contained in this manual. Regardless of what the manual says or provides, the company promises nothing and remains free to change wages, benefits, and all other working conditions, without having to consult anyone and without anyone's agreement; and the company continues to have the absolute power to fire anyone with or without cause. This manual is not a contract or a promise; it contains only general guidelines which the company may decide to follow in particular situations depending upon the circumstances.

VII. BOJINKA TR-707

All the exits are sealed. I have made sure of that. For things to be done right, I have to follow the plans completely. There's no slacking off or cutting corners when it comes down to business. This is *serious* business, you know. I made sure to follow every step. This isn't just a hobby. This isn't a game. I have instructions. I have plans. I have everything necessary for success. I have made sure of that. I am serious about this. I am serious about everything I do. I've been like this since I was a kid. I'm always very, very serious.

So what now?

Oh yeah. Now that the exits are sealed, I have to leave the packages in the assigned areas. This can be tricky since I don't know if any of the areas have been compromised since the planning stage. I sure hope not. As intelligent as I am, I'm actually not good when it comes to changing things at the last moment. I like things to be planned. I like things a certain way and that's that. So now comes the difficult part of making sure all the packages are in their assigned places. I will double check the exits and make sure they are sealed completely. The windows also have to be sealed no matter what size they are. Even small windows need to be sealed in order for this operation to be successful. There is really no room for mistakes. There is no room for careless errors. There's no slacking off or cutting corners when it comes down to business. This is *serious* business, you know. I take things seriously all the time. I'm not into being casual. I'm not into joking around. Everything is serious because at any given moment we are all in danger.

Tim is supposed to call me when he's ready. I'm holding my cell phone and staring at it. I expect his call to come in any minute now.

If he doesn't call I am going to assume he was murdered by one of many government assassins who have been following us for the last month or so. It must sound like I'm extremely paranoid but that's not the case. Tim has photographs of the men who have been tailing us. They are strong-looking men with dark complexions. They look Middle Eastern. They look dangerous. They want to kill me and they want to kill Tim. They will probably want to torture us first. They will hammer nails into our skulls. They will stick our heads in sewage. They will attach electrodes to our genitals. They will hold up pictures of our wives and make vile plans for them. They will threaten our children. They will promise to do terrible, terrible things to them.

I will not let them do it.

Correction. I will not let them do it before the operation is complete. Once I accomplish what I need to accomplish, then they can do what they want to because it won't matter. It'll be finished.

I'm staring at my phone. Come on, Tim. Call me. Call me so I know you got it all done. I can't do this alone and all the exits are sealed.

VII. EXITS EXIST

Jessica puts a VHS tape into the VCR.

Six hours of home movies. Six hours of family time she does not remember. The video cassette is a document of a time before the tragedy, the time before her father jumped from that building.

The home video footage is in the point-of-view of her father. He was the one who bought the video camera and was the one who always insisted on recording family events. Because of that, he is hardly in any of the movies. Jessica watches her life from her father's eyes.

The family outside having a picnic. The family at the park. The family opening Christmas presents. The family relaxing in the pool. The family at the zoo. The family in the backyard.

Jessica watches as her father zooms in on her mother and her as they play with the dog. The camera zooms out and tilts upwards. It zooms in on something in the sky: an airplane. Zooms in, zooms in. Shaky but focused on the plane. Jessica hears her own young voice say, "Daddy, did you see what I did? Did you see, Daddy?"

"Yeah, sweetie, I saw," her father replies, still focusing the camera on the plane and only the plane.

"Daddy, look!"

"I see you, Jess."

"Look, Daddy!"

"I heard you, Jess."

"Look!"

Jessica presses the PAUSE button. The screen is frozen on the plane. There are no windows on the plane. There are no markings of any kind. Jessica wonders if it's even a plane at all.

What was it?

Jessica presses PLAY and watches another minute of footage. She hears her own voice. She hears her mother's voice. She hears her father hum.

"Daddy, look!"

"I see it, sweetie."

"Look!"

"I see it."

The plane disappears in the sky. The camera shakes and stops focusing altogether. There are only blurry clouds. Her father continues to hum.

"Daddy!"

Jessica presses STOP.

She cannot watch anymore but she wonders what the rest of the tape is like. Instead of watching it, she will imagine it. She will imagine her father taking the camera with him into that hotel.

He films the walk into the lobby. He films himself paying for the room. He films the elevator ride and the walk down the hallway. He films the rug in the hallway. As a woman passes, he films her legs and shoes. He zooms in almost as if he wants the camera to somehow go up her dress. He films the hotel room door. He films himself putting the keycard into the slot. He films himself opening the door and turning on the lights. He films himself turning the television on with the filthy remote control.

Jessica watches through her father's eyes as he walks around the hotel room. He films the painting on the wall, zooming in and out on the streaks of oil paint. He films the bed sheets. He pulls the pillows off the bed and films himself throwing them against the window.

He walks to the window and films the cityscape. There is something about the city that makes Jessica ill.

It might have been the car exhaust or the pollution in general but then she thinks it is the sheer majesty of everything. The buildings do indeed seem to scrape the sky, they are frightening and godlike. They are unnatural.

The streets below the hotel are filled with heads and machines. Jessica thinks life boils down to just that: brains and machines bustling around the city like insects. She always has these thoughts. Now these are her father's thoughts as he films the city. He zooms in on taxi cabs and pedestrians chatting on cell phones.

She leans her forehead against the television, looking

at the insects below. She whispers words and wishes they were her father's words. She wishes they were slow bombs hurled out of the hotel room window. They would explode in beautiful blossoms of fire and debris. She thinks about taking off her clothes, strapping explosives to her chest, and walking through the city. She'd wait until someone approaches her and then...

Her father zooms out and points the camera at the sky. He focuses on a plane or at least that's what Jessica assumes it is. It does not have any windows or markings of any kind. She is not even sure she is seeing anything. The camera is having trouble focusing.

The camera drops.

Jessica falls to the carpet.

She rubs her forehead against the floor until it starts to burn.

"Daddy, look!"

"I see it, sweetie. I see it."

VIII. LONG SPEARS SHORT EYES

Ronald tries to hug his wife but she pushes him away and whispers something about squads of white men disguised as Middle Eastern women. They are shadowy figures with weapons. They move silently and kill quickly. They will stop at nothing to complete an assignment. They are efficient assassins. They are ghosts with guns.

"Their faces!" she says.

Ronald tries to wrap his arms around her again but fails. She runs to a box and pulls out a piece of paper. "This!"

"What, Susan?"

"This! It has your name on it!"

"Stop screaming. I'm standing right here." He walks over to her and takes the paper. It's an interoffice memo from his company. Susan is correct. It has his name on it. In fact, the entire memo is *about* him.

"What the hell is this? Where did you get this?" he

says. He is getting ill. He cannot believe what he's reading. Other than his name, none of what is in the memo looks even remotely familiar.

"I got it in the mail," his wife says. "I got it in the mail with the rest of the papers."

"The rest?" Ronald asks as his wife shoves a box full of memos that look similar to the one he is holding. They are all about him. They are not only from his company, however. They are from dozens of other companies and government agencies, most of which he has never heard of. "What the hell is this, Susan?"

"As if you don't know, Ron. As if you don't know."

"I don't. This is insane. Who sent you this stuff?"

Susan shakes her head. "I don't know his real name."

"Who?"

"Tim."

"Tim who?"

Susan shakes her head. "I don't know."

Ronald curses. He throws the papers to the ground and grabs his wife's shoulders. He doesn't want to hurt her. He's never hurt her. But he is coming close to it.

"What's happening here, Susan? Tell me. What's happening to you?"

"Nothing, Ron. I'm finally getting to the bottom of everything. I'm finally learning everything I need to know."

"This is crazy, Susan. Who's this Tim person? When did he contact you? Have you met him?"

"I don't want to talk about him anymore."

"Why not? Did he hurt you? Threaten you?"

Susan goes limp in his grasp.

Ron scans through the other memos: *Two members of the first group walk up to the truck that has been repainted recently. In black cursive script the words Mons Graupius Moving have been painted on the sides. Under the words were pictures of crudely drawn 'smiley' faces. It is Ronald. His handler has confirmed this.*

Susan falls to the floor. Her head hits the cement.

IX. DEBRIS CONTINUES TO FALL YOU COULD SEE

The doctors watch the footage.

It is being projected onto a large white sheet on the wall of the conference room.

"This Bunting person. He's good," Corbelli says. "He has *the eye*."

Sotos nods. "Yes. He is quite the talent."

Dr. Visna doesn't say a word. He is too busy watching the footage in hopes he will catch something the other men don't.

Corbelli says, "We have his services for how long?"

"Another month. Maybe less."

"He's good."

"You said that already."

"Well, I am saying it again."

"Okay."

"Is a month going to be enough time?"

Sotos nods. "Yes. I'm sure of it."

"How about you, Visna?" Corbelli says.

The third doctor throws a dismissive wave in their direction. "Wait." He is too busy watching the footage. The camera has zoomed in on an office building window. In the window there is a woman standing with her back to the camera. She is making hand gestures to someone in the room. The doctors cannot see who that someone is.

After a minute of this, the camera zooms out and pans left to focus on another window. This one is open. A man's face is clearly seen poking his head outside. He spits into the air. The camera tries to follow the spit but fails.

Visna moans. "This camera is cheap!"

Sotos says, "All cameras are the same. We are not worried about the camera. We have Bunting."

"I don't care about Bunting. That type of man is easily found elsewhere," Dr. Visna says. "I can go downtown and find ten more."

"Then do it," Corbelli says. "Then you go do that! Find ten more men! Or how about eleven? Nineteen? Find me nineteen men!"

Sotos presses PAUSE and says, "Let's not argue. So far it looks like we have almost everything we need. Another month or so and we'll be set. Bunting is fine. Yes, there are more men like him but he has particular...*qualities* that are valuable to us. The camera, well, the camera is fine, like I said. Got it?"

Visna nods. "Fine. I got it."

"Good," Sotos says. "Now let's continue."

He presses PLAY.

X. WARNING GRAPHIC CONTENT

I am standing in front of the lake.

I've driven by it before but never took the time to actually *look* at it. It's not a beautiful lake or anything. It's actually rather unattractive: greenish water that looks thick with waste. People fish in the lake, though. I'm not sure if they catch anything but they still take their little boats on the water and spend their time trying.

I've never been fishing.

I almost went as a kid but the plans fell through and so the sport always seemed remote. Now as an adult, I'm clueless as to how one would even go about fishing. I think about my father. He was the one who was going to take me fishing but he never did and I wonder if he ever went fishing when he was a kid. I never asked him. I never had any reason to, really. I probably could have asked him a lot of things about his childhood but didn't because I've always felt weird asking questions. He never volunteered a lot of information, either. Occasionally he'd tell me a story from when he was a kid but that was rare and I've forgotten most of them. He had also alluded to some sort of tragic event in his adolescence but he would never elaborate and I never felt like I could ask about it any further. I got the sense that it was something extremely humiliating. I still wonder what it was.

So I'm standing in front of the lake and looking into the dark water for fish. There are no fish as far as I could see. I pick up a stick from the ground and hold it as if it was a fishing pole. I'm just pretending. I know it is not a fishing pole and I know I will catch no fish. I am holding it in order to give myself the impression of fishing. If I had a boat I'd get into it and go out on the water to pretend. But I don't have a boat.

The silence is making me ill.

I think of my father and his decision to leave my mom and me for that cult. He called it an *organization* but everyone else called it a cult. They worshipped silence. They probably worshipped other things, too, but I never really found out too much about it. My father wanted it that way. He didn't want me involved. It was *his* thing. It was *his* organization, *his* lifestyle change. The abandonment of his family was simply the first step to his happiness, his salvation. My mother and I quickly accepted this. We had no choice, really. We got by fine on our own.

I'm holding the stick over the lake and am reminded of dowsing rods.

I am reminded of my father's aversion to horoscopes

and psychics, rock music and role-playing games. It wasn't as much as an aversion as it was a hatred for anything that he thought had to do with the occult. I wonder what he would have thought of dowsing rods. I wonder what he'd say if he saw me standing here holding a stick, pretending to fish, and thinking about dowsing rods. He would probably call it demonic. He used to call a lot of things demonic: cartoons, heavy metal music, any sort of fast dancing.

What would he think if he knew that I hate silence? What would he think if he knew I talk all the time just to spite him? I talk to everyone about anything. I talk to every one of my coworkers. I talk to strangers. I talk to telemarketers. I talk to everyone and anyone. My father can't tell me to be quiet. He can't tell me that silence is golden. I talk to anyone and everyone. I talk and I talk.

I am standing in front of the lake, pretending to fish, and I am not silent.

XI. FLOWER CONTRAILS WITH DOCTOR

"What did you seek to accomplish by checking into that hotel, Jessica?"

"I don't know."

Dr. Finn says, "I think you do."

"No."

"Jessica, if you can't admit these things then you won't be able to get better."

"I don't know why I went there. I just did."

"You know what the city does to your state of mind. You know what hotels do. Before we can go on, we have to talk about why you went there."

"I don't know. I just did."

Dr. Finn sighs. "Jessica."

"What?"

"I want to help you."

"I know."

"So you have to let me."

"I am."

"Well, we have to talk about this."

"About what?"

Dr. Finn sighs again. "About the hotel, Jessica."

"There's nothing to talk about."

"Do you want to end our session, then, or just sit in silence for the next forty minutes?"

Jessica shrugs. "I don't care."

"You're paying to be here. Might as well take advantage of it."

"Can't we just sit here?"

"What purpose do you think that would serve, Jessica?"

"I don't know."

"*I think* you believe that sitting here in silence will solve your problems."

"No. I don't think that."

"I think you do, Jessica."

"What do you want me to talk about?"

"What do you think?"

"My father."

"I think that would be a good start."

"Haven't we talked enough about him?"

"Not enough, no, especially considering your recent trip to the hotel."

"It's not a big deal, really."

"I think it is and I think *you* know it is, too."

Jessica puts her chin to her chest. She shakes back and forth. She groans.

"So I went to the hotel," she says.

"Yes…"

"I wasn't thinking of my dad when I made the reservation. I really wasn't."

"I believe you."

"But when I got there, that's all I could think about."

"Just your father?"

Jessica looks up at the doctor. "No. Other things, too."

"You mean…"

"The rape."

"In what context?"

"I thought about my father and how he wasn't there to stop it."

"Do you think that's fair?"

"What do you mean?"

"Do you think it's fair to blame your father? The fact is your father had been gone for several years when it happened and even if that hadn't been the case, do you think he'd be in the position to stop it from happening?"

"I didn't say it was a rational thought or anything. It's just what I was thinking about. I can't help but think that if he hadn't killed himself then maybe certain things wouldn't have happened that would have put me in the position to be, you know…"

"Raped."

"Yeah."

"Jessica, it wasn't anyone's fault but the man who committed the assault. You need to forgive yourself and your father."

"That's not all I was thinking about at the hotel."

"Oh?"

"I was thinking about how much I would enjoy seeing someone else die at the hotel, seeing someone else jump or something."

"I think you know that's not a healthy thought… though it's not an uncommon one in your position. You want to transfer the pain and guilt onto someone else. You want to let someone else live your life."

"No, I don't think that's it."

"Oh?"

"I honestly just want to see someone, anyone, in pain. Not just one person, either. I want to see a whole bunch of people in physical pain, emotional pain. I spent most of the night at the hotel thinking about that."

"Jessica, I think we have a deeper problem here and I think we'll have to talk about it in depth next week."

"I'm going to have to cancel next week's session."

"Oh?"

"I'm going on vacation."

"Really? Where?"

"I don't know yet."

"Jessica, you can't run away from your problems."

"I'm not."

"Then what are you doing?"

"I'm solving them."

XII. SHUTTLES

Barry and his wife kiss slowly.

He feels an erection stirring but knows not to get his hopes up. It's been weeks since anything has happened in that area. His wife's hand grabs at his crotch. More blood flows through his member. Then it ceases.

"Goddamn it. Let's just forget it," Barry says.

"Don't be like that, hon."

"This is going to take forever."

"I don't mind."

"I know," Barry says. "I just feel bad going through all of this. It's not even worth it. I'll just end up missing my orgasm anyway."

"You don't even want to try?"

"No. What's the point?"

His wife sighs. "I'm sorry, hon."

"No, *I'm* sorry."

"What about those supplements you talked about?"

"I don't know. I read about some of their side effects."

"Like what?"

"Diarrhea, dry mouth. I don't need that, too."

"So you won't even try them?"

"What's the point?"

"I think it's worth a try, Barry."

"Well, I don't."

His wife starts touching his penis again and then moves down to his scrotum. She massages it for a minute. She says, "Hmm."

"What?"

"I think I….feel something."

"Feel something? What? What do you mean?"

"Don't freak out. I just feel a little something, like a lump. It's probably nothing."

Barry pushes his wife's hand away and covers his crotch.

She says, "Feel it for yourself."

"No."

"Why not?"

"I can't." He is covering his crotch but makes sure not to touch his scrotum.

"Want me to call the doctor?"

"No."

"And you're not even going to feel it for yourself?"

"Just forget about it, okay? I don't need this now."

"I know. That's why I want you to get it checked out."

Barry leans his head back on his pillow. "And then what? I get it checked out and I end up having to get my balls cut off. Would you stay with me? I'd be half a man. Not even man at all, really. Would you stay with me?"

"Don't be ridiculous, Barry!"

"Answer the question! If I didn't have balls and if it turned out I would never be able to get hard, would you stay with me?"

"Of course and it pisses me off that you're even asking me that question."

"You can't even have sympathy for me?"

"Are you kidding? I'm telling you to go to the doctor! I care about you!"

Barry stands up and walks out of the room. He hopes his wife doesn't think he's going to call the doctor. He isn't. He isn't going to inspect himself either. He'll take her word for it that there is a growth somewhere in his scrotum. He will also assume that it is malignant. He will assume it will kill him and if it kills him, well, then that's what's going to happen.

He knows he's not going to spend any time checking his scrotum. It's a strange thing to do. It will make him feel weird and uncomfortable and it will only open himself up to more paranoia. He will not inspect his testicles. He will not.

XIII. SINKHOLES

Dr. Corbelli opens his cabinet to reveal hundreds of VHS tapes.

He has not upgraded his archives to digital versions. He enjoys the feel of the tapes, the heaviness and the sound and the smell. They are his tapes, his movies. His name was on many of them.

He pulls a tape off the shelf. Bright cursive letters spell out the title.

HAPPY BUILDINGS!

It is a copy of one of his first films. Corbelli had written the screenplay and produced it under a pseudonym. He was on the set everyday and had watched the filming of it.

It had been a good experience. The actors were attractive and pliable for the director. They accepted the screenplay, accepted their lines, accepted their place in the position of "puppets" in HAPPY BUILDINGS!

They were puppets, yes. Corbelli made sure his screenplay called for the actors to do things they wouldn't normally do. He made sure he picked a director who would follow through with the words he had written, a director who would read the subtext in the screenplay and understand what Corbelli wanted to accomplish.

The film was targeted to children.

Targeted.

All of the movies Corbelli had made were for children. He would have had it no other way. Producing those films allowed him absolute freedom while not having to conform to anyone's expectations.

He puts the movie into the VCR.

He takes the well-worn screenplay out of his desk drawer.

He presses PLAY on the VCR and as the movie plays, he reads along. The movie does not deviate from the screenplay. Corbelli smiles as the words turn into reality. The actors on screen spill his words.

"What do you expect us to do, Tim?"

"I don't know!"

"We can go down the stairs."

"I don't think that's a good idea, Jake."

"Well, the elevators are broken."

"I know."

"So what are we going to do?"

"We're going to find a way out of here, that's what!"

The sounds of fire crackling. Debris falling. Metal on metal.

"Tim!"

"I know, I know!"

"I can't see anything!"

"Me either!"

"I can't breathe!"

"Me either!"

"What are we going to do, Tim?"

"We're going to find a way out of here, that's what!"

Loud crackling of flames. Explosions.

"I can't hear anything, Tim!"

"Me either!"

"I can't hear anything, Tim!"

"I heard you, Jake!"

Corbelli presses PAUSE. Tim's face is blocked by smoke. Jake's face is engulfed in flames. Corbelli puts his face up to the television and feels the electricity tickle his nose. He presses PLAY.

"I can't hear anything, Tim! I can't see anything! I can't move! Something's got me! Something's got me real bad!"

"I heard you, Jake. I heard you."

Corbelli presses PAUSE while the screen is filled with smoke and falling debris. He begins to masturbate.

XIV. MENSTRUAL MIGHT

Ronald sits across from Dr. Visna. The doctor leans forward with his hands folded. He smiles.

"I am sorry to hear about your wife."

"Thank you," Ronald says. "I just don't know what to do. I'm pretty sure she's not taking her medication. Her behavior's getting worse."

"I know, I know. I'm sorry. It's sad, very sad. We will have to change our strategy."

"What am I going to do?"

"Well, we have a few options," Dr. Visna says. "First, we can prescribe her different medication. This is probably not the best option since she is unwilling to take her medication to begin with. Second, we can convince her to check herself into a facility."

"Facility?"

"An inpatient program at the Drake McMartin Institute. That's what I think would be best. She's obviously getting worse."

Ronald puts his hands on his head. "I don't know, I don't know."

"It may be the only way for her to get well. I've had quite a few patients who have completed the program there and they are much better now."

"What kind of facility? I don't want to send my wife to an insane asylum."

"Oh no, no! It is not an insane asylum. It's a special hospital with a special program for people who have problems similar to your wife's. I think it's the only option we have right now. But it's up to you, of course."

Ronald stands up and starts to pace around the room. "I don't know. I don't know. I don't want her to think I'm just locking her away."

"Like I said, it is not an asylum. She will not be locked up. She will be treated by a team of doctors and experts. She will be allowed to leave on her own after forty-eight hours. Before that time, however, she'll have to cooperate with the doctors and experts."

"How am I supposed to suggest this? Can you maybe talk to her about it?"

Dr. Visna nods his head. "We can do it together. Where is she now?"

"At home."

"Alone?"

Ronald nods. "She wouldn't leave the house."

"Do you think she's safe there?"

"I don't know. I didn't want to leave her but she

wouldn't go and I didn't want to get her upset."

Dr. Visna shakes his head. "I understand but I think you should go home now and convince her to come see me. If she won't, just call me and put her on the phone. I'll talk to her."

"Thank you. I'm just at the end of my rope. I don't know what to do."

"You don't have to explain. It would be difficult for anyone. But we will get her help. We will get her into that facility. I will make sure of it. She's a beautiful, beautiful woman and she deserves the best treatment."

"Thank you."

"You don't have to thank me, Ronald. I'm here to help. I'm always here to help."

XV. NETWORKS

Fuse cords, priming adaptors, flash artillery, surface trip flares, NH4NO3, CH3NO2, resinous glaze, CH3OH, Amatex, carnauba wax, Semtex, soy lecithin, C4 (LoFi), Astrolite G, argon candles, grandizer, yellow 5 lake, Voltes V, OKFOL, palm kernel, cordtex, adipic acid, red 40 lake, crospovidone, HC smokeless powder, FINN pills, PGGB lubricant, modified corn starch, magnesium stearate, talc.

XVI. LOSS OF MEMORY

This subject is too upsetting for your young children. I urge you to exercise parental discretion. We are married to the skyscrapers and fall into the honeymoon. The abuse is really happening. I believe we have to *believe* it is really happening. It is beyond what we know as human beings. It is an epidemic and our involvement in it is something we must rethink. It demands our attention. The therapists know. We have direct knowledge and we have the courage to resist the intimidation. It is a global thing. We have proof. Those bones are put into concrete barrels and sold as souvenirs. We have seen the saint as a translucent spook. You are not concerned. This subject is too upsetting for mothers and fathers and brothers and sisters and uncles and aunts and grandmothers and grandfathers and even neighbors. Are you using your philosophy as a cover for your violence? Are you using your philosophy as a way out of your situation? Are you using your philosophy to strike fear into the hearts of men and women and boys and girls? Are you using your philosophy to justify your acts of terror against me?

I stand by the window and you are running towards me like a maniac and you crash into the window and I'm covered in glassy wounds. You've made me into a martyr. You've made me into a silly victim of circumstance. I've burned bridges and made you an enemy and now you do *this*. You try to destroy me. Are you using your philosophy to make a fool out of me? Are you using your philosophy to make a fool out of yourself? It's all just a matter of time and money and time and money and fools soon parting with both. The future trembles at the very thought of my actually arguing with you over the details of your case. I do not want to defend you but sometimes I wonder if I will have to. Things happen for a reason. Things happen for no reason. I am between both worlds. I am at the mercy of your acts of terror. I am at the mercy of your mercy. You are merciful to your cities. You are merciful to your victims. This subject is too upsetting.

You are taking me somewhere. You are taking me to a lake. You are taking me to the movies. You are taking me to a big, big, big building and showing me the way to the top. You are showing me the roof. You are showing me there is nothing to be afraid of even though I am terrified of tall things and of things in the sky. It is unnatural to be this far up. It is unnatural for things to be that high in the sky. You want to finally take me fishing. The agency is blacking out my messages. Are you using your philosophy to cure me of my pain? Are you using your philosophy to teach me a lesson about loss? Are you using your philosophy to bury my memories of your acts? This subject is too upsetting for your young children. They have nightmares about the photographs. This subject is too upsetting for even me. I am not afraid of loss. I am only afraid of the memory of loss. I am only afraid of the memory of loss. I am only afraid of the memory of loss. It is too unnatural to be this far up in the sky. I must fall in order to alleviate my fears. I must fall. I must fall and you must not follow me down.

XVII. HAYMARKET OK CITIES

Tim Osman Spears orders a soda.

The waitress brings it to him, sets it on the table, and smiles. She says, "Will that be all, sir?"

Tim nods. "Yes. Thank you."

He drinks all the soda in one long gulp. He belches and takes out a small notebook from his pocket. He takes a pen out of his other pocket. He starts to write.

If I can take just a little bit of this experience and do something worthwhile, I will feel like I've accomplished something other than just sitting impotently here in some god forsaken town in a god forsaken restaurant waiting for something to hit me over the head with an idea, with a plan other than the original plan, the one plan I woke up with ten years ago today. Has it been that long? Strange. Ten years ago sounds so long but it seems like only days since I woke up and wrote down my plan for everything. So this is what it has come down to. Everyday I do the same thing. I ingest copious amounts of sugar and salt in order to turn the inside of my body into a preserved object of power, of perseverance, of intent. Sometimes I take opiates. That's what I am, really, just pure intent. What do I intend to do? I am intending to do what I originally planned to do ten years ago today. I am not a bad person. I am a good person. I like to help people. It gives me great pleasure to help people. I'm polite. I help people. I'm well-mannered. My teeth hurt, though, and sometimes I wonder if all the sugar I ingest is taking its toll. So maybe next time I will order water and only water.

"You sure that will be it?" the waitress says.

Tim looks up, startled. "Uh…"

"Some water?"

"Uh, yeah. Some water would be nice."

"Okay."

"Thank you," Tim says. He has lost his train of thought. He cannot continue writing in his notebook. He looks out the window. He picks up a spoon and looks at himself in it. He does not look like himself. The disguise he is wearing is a good one. He is glad he chose the beard and mustache. He is glad he chose the contact lenses. No one will recognize him.

He has to get back to the hotel soon. Once he drinks his water, he will pay the bill and leave. He will drive to the hotel while looking for coded messages along the way. They are often on the back of stop signs and on lampposts. They are sometimes disguised as illiterate graffiti.

When he gets to the hotel, he will take a nap on the

floor because you should never sleep on motel beds. They are dangerous in so many ways. Tim will fall asleep on the floor while looking at the crack in the ceiling. He will imagine the crack growing larger and turning into a hole that will engulf him.

Where will he be then?

That's right. He'll be following more signs, more signals.

The phone call comes in. His guy in Trenton is calling him. He's upset. He is losing patience. Tim is behind schedule.

"I'll do it soon. I'll do it tonight. I promise. It will be ready tomorrow morning. Tomorrow morning for sure."

"I don't believe you, Tim. I don't believe you. I want to believe you but I don't."

"I'm dependable. I'm reliable. I am doing everything I am supposed to do. I am dedicated. I'm a good person."

"You must dip your pen in your black ink and write your name upon their tongues, Tim. *You* know that."

"I know. I know that's what I have to do. I will do it. I will do it tomorrow. I will do it tomorrow morning. The sun will rise tomorrow morning."

"It will rise and it will blind them. Right?"

"Yes, it will blind them."

"Get to work."

"Okay."

Tim thinks he might be in the wrong business.

XVIII. OUTSIDE JOB

My father is a pilot. He is a reasonable man. He is a normal man. He is a pilot. He has no reason to lie to me. He has no reason to lie to anyone.

I cannot be sure of his motives in telling me the complete truth. I'd expect him to hide some of the details from me. I am his child and I'd expect he would want to shield me from the unsavory details associated with the so-called acts of terror. I didn't want to know the whole truth. I was perfectly content reading comic books and watching cartoons. I was perfectly content building forts out of pillows and blankets. I didn't want to think about the truth.

There is no conspiracy. My father is a reasonable man. He tells me the truth. He tells me everything there is to know about societal ills. Everything is so completely random, so complex, it comforts our brains to assume there are secrets behind the acts. The terror plot is really hundreds of random plots from hundreds of authors working in the dark, working in the fallout shelters built by paranoid billionaires. None of the authors know any other authors even exist. Each author believes that he or she is the only author alive creating these plots, weaving them through other plots. They have a massive collection of plot twists and secrets and bizarre characterizations and obscure allusions. They randomly place act after act within subplots and back-stories. They have no awareness other than their own plots. I know *all* of these plots. I am in each and every plot and so is my father. My father is the father of these plots. He is the father of the authors and of each back-story and footnote. I am a footnote. I am an index to my father's obsessions. I walk through each plot and destroy it with my treacherous tongue.

"You don't know what you're saying," you say. "You talk bullshit with nothing to back it up. You talk about some generalized plotting but you have nothing to back it up. I call that bullshit."

"You're probably right," I say. "You are probably right and that's why I am filled with hatred for the truth and hatred for my father for *telling* me the truth. If he had just kept his mouth shut then perhaps I'd just be sitting in a different room in a different house in a different town without having to worry about all these plots and all the dangerous things."

"So just leave already," you say. "Just leave and forget about your father and his precious plots."

"He's not the one behind the plots," I say.

You nod. "Sure. Yeah right."

"It's true," I say. "It's true. Despite my hatred for him, I won't let you accuse him of that. He's really done nothing wrong outside of the house. He doesn't have any friends. He doesn't have a social life."

"And you hate him?" you say. "And you *hate* him."

"I do. But that's not the point," I say. "I'd probably find some reason to hate him no matter what. It's a way of dealing with my own insecurities as a son. It's a way to excuse my own shortcomings. It's perfectly normal. You believe me, right?"

"I believe *you* believe it's normal," you say. "I believe you are fine with it but that doesn't mean I'm going to cut your father slack. You really need to leave the house more often, see the world, get a chance to talk to people."

"I talk to people," I say.

"I know you do," you say. "I know you do."

"I do," I say.

"And your father," you say. "What about your father?"

"My father is a pilot," I say. "He is a reasonable man. He is a normal man. He is a pilot. He has no reason to lie to me. He has no reason to lie to anyone."

"Your father is a liar," you say. "I know this to be true."

"My father is a pilot," I say. "He is a reasonable man. He is a normal man. He is a pilot. He has no reason to lie. He has no reason to lie to anyone."

XIX. YOUR CITY IS OK

Barry puts on the cassette tape titled *OK CITY, OK! HAP-PY 1995.*

It's all just noise.

He imagines his wife trying to seduce him to the sounds. He imagines her reading from the booklet as a way to arouse his penis. He imagines it does not work. After all, nothing will work. Even in his fantasies.

It's not her fault. Barry knows this and hopes she does, too. He imagines that someday someone will find a medicine that will cure him of this unfortunate situation. He's had enough of defeat. He's had enough of disappointment.

The noise shakes him. Walls falling into floors and ceilings falling into walls. Metal on metal on metal on metal. Sheetrock and rumbling and fire and screaming that sounds like the walls falling. Radio broadcasts buried underneath the roar.

He reads the booklet that came with the cassette. Black and white pictures. Blurry typed paragraphs. Smudged ink. Diagrams.

The noise lulls him into submission as he reads.

XX. OK BOOKLET

OK? I want to be totally self-confident in direct proportion to the objection with the description my father gave me of how he got the scar on his side being a "snake bite" and a "birth mark" to myself after proof of truth that it was really a scar from a gunshot to me personifying about the scar psychologically imposing me being (1) the cause of the bruise (2) the after memory of the scar (3) and the amount of thought it took to protect me from the worry and fear and guilt I later found I took upon myself "being" a "bookmark" between my father and grandfather's action, journal of the wise and unwise actions they took for themselves that later were inflicted on me…being called the "bruiser" by a nurse on the day I was born in Marburg Hospital located in the CITY of Plainfield where my father was injured by that bullet while on duty before I was born. OK? I want to remember what side Tim Spears said I was on when he first saw me in the sub shop when he used to work while he was holding a push broom in his right hand back in the early 1980s. OK? I want to be totally self-confident in direct relation to how hazardous Tim Spears thought

I was when he worked at the sub shop in Dunellen. OK? I want to be totally self-confident in direct proportion to how psychologically threatening of a munchkin to him having to handle his suppression he imposes on himself and me since the first time he 2nd guessed a purpose in his control. OK?

XXI. COLLAPSE

Dr. Sotos is sitting at his desk, fingering pill boxes. It is the last of his Taborica samples and he wants to savor them. If he wants more, he'll have to go through great lengths and he is not prepared to do that just yet.

He opens one box, pops out two pills, and looks at them in his palm. They look like small blue pebbles. He loves them. He thinks Taborica is the best medication ever developed. Dr. Sotos doesn't know what he would do without it. His marriage would have been destroyed. His children would have been killed. If it hadn't been for Taborica, his life would be in ruins.

He swallows them dry, and picks up the phone. He dials a random number. He clears his throat.

When someone answers, Dr. Sotos says, "Hello, is Mickey there?"

"No, sorry, wrong number."

"No, really, is Mickey there? This is Mickey's Donut

Shop, right?"

"Wrong number," the person says and hangs up.

Sotos giggles. He dials another random number.

"Hello?"

Sotos says, "Is Tim there?"

"Sorry, wrong number."

"Can I speak to Tim, please?"

The person hangs up.

Sotos laughs and dials a third random number. When the person picks up, he coughs into the phone and says, "There's nothing we can do *at the moment* but you should wait patiently like *a good little girl*."

"Who is this?"

"It's Tim, my dear," Sotos says. "We met at the office."

"I think you have the wrong number."

"I have all the *right* numbers."

The person hangs up.

This time Sotos does not laugh. His nostrils flare and he pops two more pills out of the sample box and swallows them dry.

He dials another number but this one is not random. He knows exactly who he is calling.

"Hello?" the person says.

"Dad?"

A heavy sigh on the other line. "What?"

"It's me."

"I know who it is. What do you want?"

"I just wanted to talk."

"About what? I'm busy."

"I don't know. I figured we could just *talk*."

"We don't have anything to say to each other."

"Dad, please…"

"What? If you have something to say, just say it."

"I'm dying, Dad."

"Not this again!"

"Dad, I am!"

"No, you're not. I'm not dealing with this again. Neither is your mother. Don't call again until you get some help, some *real* help."

Sotos sobs into the phone. He waits for his father to say something but he waits in vain. Finally he says, "Dad? You still there?"

"Yes."

"Can I come see you and mom?"

A heavy sigh. "No."

"Why not?"

"Because."

"Why?"

"You'll upset your mother and I'm not having her go through that again. Don't call. Don't visit. Once you get help, then maybe."

"I don't need help. I need *you*."

"No, no. You're not putting this on me. You're not putting the responsibility on me. Not again. I'm sick of this. I'm hanging up now, okay? I'm hanging up. Don't call back."

"Dad!"

The line goes dead.

Sotos opens another box of Taborica and takes four more pills.

XXII. SUPER ACTION NOISE BUILDING BLACK

Review from the August 1998 issue of *ORANGECOD* magazine:

OK CITY, OK! HAPPY 1995 / C-60 / Hideo Institute

This self-titled cassette was released by the same label that gave us the SCOP series of tapes that documented the Iranian-American noise scene in NYC. This tape, however, does not list the person or persons who recorded it. The insert is minimal with only a black-and-white photocopy of a smiley face superimposed over a demolished building. That being said, I have heard that some copies came with a booklet. That's a shame because I imagine it would have shed some light on the sounds on the tape. Anyway, the noise presented here is rather typical of the scene. Low-end bass noise, crunchy explosion sounds, metal-on-metal noise, contact mic freak-out, etc. It's dynamic, yes, but nothing that makes it stand out from the hundreds of other noise cassettes being released. There are a few moments where I could hear voices under the sounds. I wouldn't say they were vocals really, more like field recordings or samples or something. Anyway, maybe if I had the booklet, I'd know more. So yeah, this is an average release but not essential to your noise collection. It's not the first of its kind and it won't be the last. Of that I'm sure: it won't be the last.

-Walter Martin

XXIII. BLACK MARY

Someone once told me the hotel was primed for demolition. Like always, I had responded with skepticism.

It just doesn't make any sense. Building the damn thing
had taken such a long time. I should know. My father was
one of the contractors. For years he would come home
from work everyday and tell my mother and me about it.
It eventually caused me to make sure I wasn't home at
dinnertime. I needed to be out of the house and out of
earshot of my father talking about it. My mother, on the
other hand, had no escape. She didn't have a driver's li-
cense and she didn't have any friends. Where was she going to go?

So because it took so long to build, I can't imagine
the building being prepared for destruction. Personally I
wouldn't put much work into something if I knew that
sometime soon it would be destroyed. I guess, in a way,
I want everything to be eternal. At the very least, I'd like

everything to outlive me. I don't want to see the end of things. Let me be the first to go. Let me be ignorant of the end of everything else.

Now, the reason why my father lost his job, well, there are a lot of rumors about that and I need to clarify some things. First, when the entire thing happened, he was actually not head of the project but was acting in a purely *supervisory* position. That may not sound like a big difference to you but I can assure you that it is. A supervisory position in that field is more of an honorary title and doesn't come with many responsibilities.

Two, at the time of the incident, my father was in the hospital undergoing gallbladder surgery. Both before and after that surgery, he was in no position to take part in even the most minimal responsibilities associated with his *honorary* supervisory position.

The last reason is one that I wasn't going to divulge but in light of recent events, I am going to have to do so. The last reason is this: for the past year or so, my father's mental state has been deteriorating rapidly. His coworkers and his immediate family members were aware of it. I wouldn't go so far as to call it a dirty secret, though. A lot has been made of some sort of "dirty secret" roaming around in my family's closet but that's not the case. I can assure you. We were just hoping that we'd somehow find some solution to his condition. My sister and I were researching medications and experimental treatment for his symptoms. My mother was looking into herbal and other holistic remedies. My father was clueless about the whole thing. He made no indication that he was aware of his symptoms.

So those are the three reasons why I do not believe that my father should be held accountable for the incident. The so-called evidence found in his house and, more specifically, on his computer does not implicate him in any way when taking into account the information I've provided above.

Other than what I've stated above, I have no comment.

XXIV. PENTEGRAM MOSK BLACK

Barry remembers the VHS tape he bought at *Hideo Video*.

His wife isn't home so he has the entire house to himself. He takes the video out of the case. XNOYBIS SUPER TERRORIST FORCE SIX. He puts it into his VCR. He presses PLAY.

What had the Japanese man said about the movie? Oh yes, the man had said, "Very exciting, action, things go BOOM. Pretty girls, tough men, evil demons, guns, BOOM!" Barry looks forward to everything but the pretty girls. He does not want to be reminded of his impotence.

The movie is quite grainy and Barry assumes it is a second or third generation bootleg. It is a widescreen version of the movie, however, and that alleviates some of his disappointment.

Bright green and yellow Japanese letters splash onto the screen. Barry assumes they spell out the title but there are no subtitles to let him know for sure.

He watches as the camera flies over a Japanese city (Tokyo?) and finally focuses on the rooftop of a building where two men in suits are arguing. Again, there are no subtitles and Barry is left to his imagination to figure out what is being said.

"What danger, Edward? What are you talking about? Why are you being so paranoid?" the older of the two men says.

"I'm not being paranoid, Tim," the other man says.

"Yes, yes you are. This always happens and I'm getting tired of dealing with it."

"So that's that? You don't believe me? That this place is dangerous?"

"Dangerous? Everywhere is dangerous, Eddie. Everywhere."

Cut to a flashback. The younger man (Eddie) is sitting with his eyes closed, presumably praying to the small pile of rubble. There is a loud sound from outside. Eddie's eyes open. He gets to his knees and crawls to the window and looks out.

A monstrous cloud of smoke engulfs most of the sky. Eddie screams. The flashback is over.

"A poison cloud!" Eddie says.

"Absurd!" Tim says.

"Death squads!"

"Even more absurd!"

"You never believe me!"

"Eddie," the older man says. A gunshot sounds and blood spurts from his chest. There are explosions on the soundtrack. There are screams.

Eddie screams as well.

He runs to the end of the roof and looks down. The camera gets a point-of-view shot of Eddie looking down at the sidewalk. Close-up of his face. He closes his eyes and mumbles something, probably a prayer. He jumps.

Barry presses PAUSE.

He hears his wife open the front door.

XXV. BLACK ASPIRIN

Jessica leaves Dr. Finn's office and goes to the hardware store. She takes a piece of paper out of her pocket and looks it over.

100 feet of zinc plated double loop chain.

8 rolls of duct tape.

40 feet of wire rope.

Latex-free gloves.

Bolt cutters.

23 inch hatchet.

1000 feet of NM-B cable.

She looks around at the other customers and at their angry eyes. They stare at her. Jessica knows it isn't her imagination. She isn't being paranoid. They are indeed gazing at her. They probably know the contents of her list.

Because of that, she is deciding to give up the plan. It was a stupid plan to begin with. It's so naïve. She needs another plan.

Jessica crumples the list and sticks it in her pocket. She walks out of the hardware store and onto the sidewalk. Traffic is stuck in front of the store and dozens of cars are idling near her. Jessica stands petrified. She knows someone in one of those cars must know who she is and what she's been doing. One of them might even be an old coworker of her father's.

If she can only figure out if this is the case, then maybe she can ask them about her father. Why did he really commit suicide? What was he working on prior to his death? Was the government responsible for it? Jessica has many questions she needs answered. She knows someone must possess that knowledge. Someone out there is hiding the secrets of her father's descent. If she can only figure it out…

Jessica steps into the road and stands in front of a taxi. The driver beeps. Jessica raises her arms above her head and shouts gibberish.

She remembers PLAN B and goes back to her apartment. Underneath her bed is her old backpack from high school. Inside she finds what she needs.

The syringe.

Jessica is fine with just a syringe.

She is just fine.

She will walk through the city and illuminate the satanic insects that have been wreaking havoc on her mental state. They have no right to remind her of her father, to remind her of the rape, to remind her of the life she had to abandon.

So she is just fine with a syringe.

It won't be as cataclysmic as she had hoped but it will get the job done and illuminate (and destroy) the seeds of her sickness. It won't be apocalyptic but it will heal the psychological wounds that continue to rot. It will be an introduction to the final plan.

The syringe is fine.

Lucky for Jessica, the city streets are crowded. There are so many people oblivious to her pain…but not for long. The world will come crashing down into their blood-stream like tainted aircraft.

Jessica leaves her apartment building. She breathes in the city air. It smells like car exhaust and hot asphalt, perfume and dog shit.

She pulls the syringe out of the bag and holds it like a knife. She spots a young man with a sketchpad and slowly walks towards him.

She gets him.

The young man reacts by smiling nervously as he is stuck by the syringe. He looks into Jessica's eyes and winces. He now knows her intentions.

Jessica walks away and sticks someone else, a middle-aged woman pushing a stroller. The woman screams. Jessica sticks the baby, too. It cries.

There are more screams and shouts. A man is yelling from a car. No one interferes, though. Jessica gets five more people before she runs three blocks and steps into a corner store. Her heart is beating hard. Her throat is dry. She sticks the person behind the counter. She grabs things off the shelves and throws them to the floor. She rips magazines into pieces. She leans her forehead against the glass, looking at the insects outside. She whispers words and wishes they were bombs.

XXVI. AGE DIFFERENCE

Barry is sitting across from his cousin Tina.

"You sure you want to go through with this?" he says.

"Yeah, of course."

"I don't know. It sounds like a risky procedure."

"I think all surgeries are risky. I just can't go on like this."

"I understand. I'm just worried."

"I appreciate that."

Barry nods. "So…what time tomorrow?"

"Seven in the morning," Tina says. "So what about you? No offense, but you don't look so good."

Barry shrugs.

"What's wrong?" Tina says.

"A whole lot of stuff really. My health is just bad, you know and it's taking a toll on everything."

"It's affecting your marriage?"

"Yeah…"

"You guys seeing someone? A counselor or something?"

Barry shakes his head. "No. I don't think that would help anyway. It's more of a problem with *me*. I'm not, you know….fulfilling my marital responsibilities if you know what I mean."

Tina nods. "Have you seen a doctor about that? You're young. I'm sure they can do something."

"The doctor gave me something but it didn't help. Honestly I'm afraid of telling him that. I'm afraid of what that'll lead to."

"What do you mean?"

"You know, like if that didn't work then that means my problem might be more serious."

"That's exactly why you need to tell him!"

"I'd rather be in the dark about it, to be honest."

"That's silly, Barry."

"I know."

They sit in silence and sip their drinks. Finally Tina puts her hand on Barry's. "Thanks for being there for me. I appreciate it."

"Of course," Barry says. "And thank you for listening. It means a lot and I think I actually feel better about things."

Tina nods. "I'm glad."

"Well, I have to get going. I have to go to work and I'm already late."

"Isn't your boss going to be mad?"

"Yeah, probably," Barry says. "But I don't know if I even care anymore."

XXVII. MONS GRAUPIUS INTERNATIONAL, LLC

The contract with Henwich & Bingen, well, that was a result of my oversight. I will admit that now. But you have to understand that in a week's span I may have ten to fifteen such contracts cross my desk and though I try to mentally digest them all, sometimes things do get by without my knowledge.

Please understand I'm not making excuses. I have taken full responsibility which is evident in my stepping down from my position in my own company, the company I helped build from the ground up. I have *zero* reasons to lie about my involvement. Hell, it wasn't even involvement but, like I said, just an oversight and for that I have apologized profusely.

Where does that leave me?

I don't know.

I'm sort of in limbo right now, trying to look for

a position that would suit me as well as help me provide for my family. Luckily, the controversy surrounding the contract with Henwich & Bingen has not sullied my reputation. Those who know me or know *of* me are well aware of my long-standing integrity.

Think about it. If I didn't possess a high level of integrity, would I have really admitted my role in this fiasco? *Certainly not.* Many men in my position would have denied until the very end. They would have found a loophole, found a way out of this whole mess. In fact, I have had several chances to do just that. But did I choose the low road? *Certainly not.* I could not live with myself, could not live with my conscience (that dweller on the threshold) if I had done so.

What you are witnessing now is one man's testimonial of repentance and of a moving forward to a brighter future. My accomplishments of the past will be rubble compared to my future. I will build a bigger, brighter, and more substantial future for my family and for me.

And no, I will not give interviews. I have found that the question-and-answer format always leaves me feeling ambushed. No matter who is asking the questions, I am always in the position of victim and not by my own choice. I hate playing the victim. I do not see myself as such. However, when being interviewed, I feel as if I am being verbally attacked and accused of a multitude of things. In those situations, I have had to talk my way out of the interview and that usually meant ending it early and with some negative feelings left between the interviewer and me. It usually leaves me rather angry. I do not like being put in the role of victim. I repeat: I do not like being forced into the role of victim. I will not be accused of things. I will not be the one being interrogated. Most of my training involves my being in the role of interrogator.

Okay, so I am admitting my responsibility in the manner and as I said above, I am looking at the various opportunities that have recently arisen. One such opportunity is with my father's company, the Butto Butto Corporation. Normally I wouldn't consider getting into business with family but under the circumstances I think it may not be a bad idea. Family relations aside, I would be beneficial to the company and in return, it would allow me the chance to build my career and build my future. I need a bigger, brighter future to quiet my critics. The best revenge is living well, right? That's how the saying goes. My critics have tried to destroy me both financially and psychologically but they haven't succeeded. If anything, they have strengthened my resolve and now I have the freedom to get stronger, smarter, and more successful. I should really thank them for it.

As for my father, he personally invited me to take a position in his company which was surprising considering that he and I have never had a close relationship. Ironically, it resembled a business relationship more than a father-and-son one. That has always been okay with me because I'm not one to coddle my emotional side. Life is business and business is life. Keep in mind

I'm not talking about money. I'm talking about business. Even if money wasn't involved, I'd still be a businessman. It's a way of life. It's a belief system. It's a moral code. It is the chariot I choose to ride.

Though we have never talked about it, I imagine my father believes the same thing. He is a pure, unadulterated businessman. He doesn't quit. I admire him but not in the way a son usually admires his father. I admire him in the way one businessman admires another. I think that's a superior form of admiration because it is not based on an emotional or nostalgic need to connect. It is totally objective.

Okay, so, with that being said, the contract with Henwich & Bingen was a result of my oversight. I am admitting that *now*. I hope this clears everything up for you and please don't hesitate to get back to me if you need anymore information on the matter.

XXVIII. HOMELAND

Barry is worried about his job.

He is sitting in his cubicle, waiting for his manager to come by and ask him why Barry's work isn't up to his usual standard. It has to happen. The company is adamant about making sure every employee works up to their standards. Every employee must follow company policy, must follow protocol. Policy is the most important thing. Policy and then profits. Without policy, there will be no profits. It is all about policy and procedure. It is about protocol. You must follow protocol or else, what's the point?

Barry sits at his desk, glancing side to side. He puts his fingers on the keyboard of his computer and types randomly. He isn't actually working. His impotence has spread from his groin to his brain. He simply *cannot work*.

Normally he is able to work through whatever personal problems come up but today he cannot do it.

As he glances around, he notices two men walking towards his cubicle. Their shirts are emblazoned with the word SECURITY. These are not subtle men.

"Sir?" the taller of the men says.

"Yeah?" Barry says.

"We need you to come with us."

"Why?"

The other man speaks. "Sir, we really need you to come with us."

"What's this about?"

"Sir…"

"Look, if this is about my work, uh, you know…"

"Come with us, sir."

Barry puts his hand on the phone. "I'd like to call my manager first."

"Sir, we're not with your company."

"What do you mean? Who are you with?"

"Sir, you'll need to come with us right now."

Barry's body stiffens. He has never been in trouble. "I don't feel comfortable without knowing what this is about first."

"Once you come with us, you'll know what this is about."

"I want to talk to my manager first."

"He knows all about it. Now, just come with us."

The taller man grabs Barry's arm. It is a gentle grab, almost reassuring. He lowers his mouth to Barry's ear and says, "Don't make a scene. Everything will be okay, sir."

Barry stands up with the man's arm still on his shoulder. He feels better with the man touching him and wonders if perhaps they are here to protect him.

The three men walk down the hallway, passing Barry's coworkers who watch out of the corners of their eyes. They are curious as to what is happening to the quietest man in the office.

At the end of the corridor, the men open the door to an empty conference room. They lead Barry to a chair and once he sits, they take seats on the other side of the table.

The taller man says, "Sir, we need to ask you a few questions."

"About what?" Barry says. "Do I need a lawyer?"

The other man laughs. "I don't believe that's necessary."

"Well, can I have my manager come in here?"

"I don't think that would be appropriate considering..."

"Considering what?"

The taller man says, "Considering the nature of our questions. It would be in your best interest *not* to have anyone else here. Also, please understand that it is beneficial to *you* if you answer the questions without hesitation."

Barry shakes his head. "I'm confused."

"There's no need to be," the other man says. "It's just a handful of questions and if you answer them honestly, this meeting will be over shortly and you can go back to work."

Barry shrugs his shoulders. "Okay, but I'd still like to know what this is all about."

The tall man's cell phone rings. He grabs for it and says to Barry, "Just a moment, sir."

The tall man answers the phone. "Yes? Yes, he's here. No, no problem. Yes, most likely. Say again? Interesting. I wasn't aware. And is that from Chicago or Boise? Well, I don't know. I'll call you back after we're done. Okay." He puts his phone away and smiles at Barry. "Sorry, sir."

Barry says, "Was that about me?"

"No, sir. It was not."

"I don't believe you."

"You don't have to believe me. Your belief has no effect on the reality of the phone call."

"You still haven't told me what this is about."

"Sir, I'm going to need you to calm down."

Barry's eyes widen. "I *am* calm! What are you talking about?"

The other man gets up and walks to Barry. "Sir, please…" He puts his hand on Barry's shoulder but it is not a reassuring touch. It is a tight, threatening grab.

"You're hurting me!" Barry says. "Stop!"

"Sir, calm down. We need you to calm down so we can ask your some questions."

"Well, then ask them. What are you waiting for?"

"We're waiting for you to calm down."

"I'm calm. I'm about as calm as I'm going to be under the circumstances. Don't you understand that?"

"We do. But you still have to cooperate."

"I am."

"Tell us why you bought five airline tickets yesterday."

"Wait, who are you? You're not building security, are you?"

"No, we are not."

"Then who the hell are you?"

"Answer the question, sir."

"I'm not answering anything. Not without a lawyer."

"You don't need a lawyer."

"I have a right to one, though."

"No, actually you do not."

"What? What the hell do you mean?"

"Under the circumstances, you do *not* have the right to an attorney."

"That's bullshit."

"No, that's the law, sir. Now, answer the question. The airline tickets. You bought five of them under questionable circumstances. We'd like some sort of explanation for this before we go any further."

"I have nothing to say."

"Silence is guilt. Let's do this the easy way. Just answer the question honestly and we'll just go on from there and hopefully have things settled in no time."

"No."

"How long have you worked in the city, Barry?"

"I'm not talking to you guys."

"How often do you leave the city on business?

How many times per month to you travel by plane? Do you usually travel alone? How many bags do you usually bring? How many carry-on bags? What hotels do you frequent? Have you ever had a fear of flying? Have you ever been treated for mental illness? Have you any grievances against your government or any other government? Have you ever experienced any sexual malfunction?"

"This is ridiculous!"

The man squeezes Barry's shoulder.

"Get your hand off me!" Barry says.

"Sir!" the taller man says, getting up and joining his partner. He grabs Barry's other shoulder and squeezes.

Barry raises his hand to resist but loses consciousness.

XXIX. WATERS

"We specialize in providing companies like yours a reliable supply of global stabilizing professionals. It's a full spectrum operation."

"I'm interested but I just don't know if it's in the budget. I just don't think I can get it approved."

"Totally understandable. But consider our competitors. Yes, the prices they give you may seem more affordable but in the long run you'll be paying more because they simply do not provide the sort of multinational peacekeeping program that we do. To be blunt, there is going to be more of a clean up after they're done. That costs more."

"Well, to be honest, cost is not my only concern."

"Oh?"

"There has been mention of the Tehran incident."

"That's to be expected but I assure you that's behind us."

"There's still a lot of media coverage and I'm afraid

that's going to affect our decision."

"Totally understandable. But consider our perspective. We did our best to fulfill a contract and it resulted in an unfortunate turn of events. We cannot be held accountable for random acts that are unforeseen. We try our best to look at every angle of every situation but sometimes that's just not possible. The media has blown this out of proportion with help from our competitors and their political allies. It would be quite unfortunate if you held that against my company."

"I know. I'm just trying to be as transparent as possible and let you know that there are a few things we'll be looking at when we decide on the contract."

"Totally understandable. I respect the thought you are putting into your decision. I assure you, though, that you will find no better company that specializes in our field. I would stake my job and my reputation on that. Trust me. I've worked for other companies and have friends who still do and I know how our record compares to theirs."

"I'll take that into consideration."

"Please do. And if you allow me, I'll say this one thing about that incident. I was a supervisor there when it happened and was eyewitness to some of the so-called acts that were committed by my men. It is not as the media has portrayed it. That coverage was so far from the truth as to make it almost science fiction, some sort of alternate reality. It angers me to think that a reasonable man like you has to be subjected to such biased news coverage of something that is both tragic and misinterpreted."

"I'll take that into consideration. But I have seen a good amount of footage."

"Oh? I hope you have not seen the versions edited by our critics."

"I've seen enough. But again, I'll take what you're saying into consideration."

"Please do. It's totally understandable for you to have some trepidation about working with us but I hope you'll keep an open mind."

"I'll have to check with the board. The decision isn't solely up to me, obviously."

"If it was, what would your decision be?"

"I don't think I could give you an answer as of yet."

"What would it take to convince you personally?"

"I honestly couldn't say."

"I have statistics if that's what you're looking for."

"No, statistics never satisfy me."

"Did I neglect to give you any information you need? If so, please don't hesitate to ask. I will provide anything I can."

"I appreciate that. I think I'll have to get back to you, though. Later this week, perhaps."

"No sooner?"

"I don't think that will be possible."

"Totally understandable. But please consider getting in touch with the references I've provided. I'm sure they will enlighten you."

XXX. MAGIC LANTERNS

Dr. Corbelli stares at the television and watches the animals.

He barely remembers making the film. He thinks it might have been thirty-five years ago but he cannot be sure. It was three weeks out of his life but he only has a fuzzy recollection.

Getting the animals to do what the screenplay had called for was a difficult task. They had trainers, yes, but the trainers consisted of ex-zookeepers who were either alcoholics or junkies or both. The other thing he remembers is the dubbing of the actors' voice in post-production. He himself had provided one of the voices…that of a duck named Timmy.

Corbelli watches the film for the first time in at least three decades. It is not so much a film as it is a splicing together of scenes of farm animals running around with humans providing nonsensical dialogue to explain the action. But children loved it. They loved the cute little animals and their antics. Corbelli remembers that much.

Now he remembers something else.

After the filming, the animals were slaughtered. They were eaten by the cast. Yes, Corbelli remembers that. He had eaten the duck he had provided the voice to. It was delicious or at least that's how he remembers it. Did it really happen? Maybe he had just fantasized about slaughtering the animals. Maybe the memory is a false one. But it *could* be true.

He also remembers making five more similar films, all with talking animals and low budgets. Why had he been involved in that? Money, yes. Money and access to filmmaking equipment in order to make his *other* movies.

It all comes back to him. He remembers the demolition films he produced. He remembers the nights he spent filming and the mornings he spent editing. He remembers the demolitions. He remembers the rubble.

He remembers the assassinations.

It is all behind him, though. He forgives himself and he forgives the films. They are the innocent offspring of a turbulent time. They cannot be blamed for what he did and he cannot be blamed for what he had been paid to do under duress. But was it really under duress? He hadn't argued against it. He hadn't refused. He had taken the job and made lots of money.

The films were to be incantations for the men who had hired him. They would use them to write history, to set up new chapters of violence and devastation and murder and messages hidden inside the skull of a prisoner of war left in a camp to rot. Yes, Corbelli had been to one of those camps. He had even *trained* at one of those camps. He learned many skills, most of which were not related to medicine or filmmaking. At the camps, he did many bad things.

But he forgives himself. Corbelli forgives himself for that and for everything because every action was an experiment. All experiments and their results deserve forgiveness.

Corbelli watches the talking duck. It was an annoying animal to work with. It was uncooperative and constantly defecated during filming.

Corbelli watches the duck waddle through a carnival funhouse as he hears his own voice shout the dialogue in a high pitched voice.

"We're all in danger! Quack! Quack!"

XXXI. THE TRICK IS NOT PERFECT

My coffee cup slides across the desk and my paperclips fall to the floor. Someone looks out the window and shouts.

There is something out there. I can see it in my peripheral vision. I won't look, though. I refuse to give in to peer pressure. I do not like or respect my coworkers and I have no interest in what they are interested in.

That being said, I'm curious.

What is it? What is causing my coworkers to stop what they are doing and put their faces to the windows? No, no, I won't get sucked into their nosiness. They just want something to talk about. They want something to break up the monotony of their day. So be it. But I will not be seduced by their behavior.

I am concentrating on my work. I am typing names into the computer.

Edward Lytton. Timothy Spears. Barry Bayley. These

are men I don't know but I have to put their names into several programs, spreadsheets, and databases. I have to fill out physical forms, too. You'd think that in the computer age we would stop using pen and paper but that's not the case. I still have to put these names on forms and fill out all the other appropriate information and then make copies, too, just in case one of them gets lost on the way to its destination. They get filed in several different places. I have to fax copies over to another department who will then fax them over to yet another department. That last department then checks with me to make sure the forms they've received are accurate.

But the names mean nothing to me. After a while they are just visual white noise. I notice there are no women's names and that disturbs me not because I'm any sort of feminist but because typing men's names over and over is making me jaded. It's like I absorb their masculine qualities with each keystroke. It's unnerving and unnatural.

Edward Lytton. Timothy Spears. Barry Bayley. Over and over again. Edward Lytton. Timothy Spears. Barry Bayley. My fingers glide over the keyboard, clicking and clicking the sigils into reality. In my mind the names become combined. Barry Spears. Edward Bayley. Timothy Lytton.

My coworkers are still at it, shouting and screaming. What does someone have to do to have a nice and quiet working environment?

Every day is exactly like the previous day. That's not

always a bad thing, really. Sometimes it's comforting to know what to expect but in my case, it's just one long prison sentence.

No, I take that back. My office is nothing like prison. I say that because I'm spoiled. I have the luxury of choice but I complain about those choices. This is nothing like prison. I can get up and leave if I want. I can go out and get lunch. I can stop what I'm doing right now and read a magazine. Sure, my boss might come over and tell me to get back to work but that's not a prison-like consequence. It's not like I'm thrown into solitary confinement for not complying. The worst I would get would be a simple talking to in my manager's office. That's it. It's nothing. My perception is often skewed because I'm a spoiled brat.

Regardless, I still can't stand my coworkers. I come into the office each morning and try to avoid as many people as I can. However, when confronted with a greeting, I reciprocate. I do so very politely and with a smile on my face. I wouldn't go so far as to call it fake, though. My goal isn't to make anyone feel bad. My goal is to come to the office, do my work, and go home with minimal interaction with anyone else.

There's a loud sound from the floor below me. It's a slow groan, loud and powerful enough to move my chair back. I am determined not to panic like the rest of my coworkers. If I do that, then I just become one of them and I will be sucked into their behavior pattern. I do not want that so I will just ignore them until everything quiets down. Then I'll finish my work and leave the office as quietly as I can. If someone says goodbye to me, well, then I will say it right back but with no eye contact. I will just keep walking. I will keep walking down the hallway and into the elevator. I will take the elevator down to the lobby and walk through the lobby and out through the main doors. I will walk right outside without making eye contact with anyone. If someone says hello or goodbye, I will say it right back to them but with no eye contact. If someone tries to start a conversation, I will politely tell them I am in a rush and I will keep on walking.

There's the slow groan again. It is more powerful than the first one. What is happening here?

What is happening?

Thanks to my medication, I am not screaming at my coworkers right now. Thanks to the recent increase in dosage, I am not leaving right now, not screaming down the hallway on my way to the elevator. I am not jumping out of a window. I am not smashing my head with my fists. I am not trying to rattle the little marbles in there.

Everything is shaking now.

All my coworkers are making noise as I am trying to type names into my computer. Edward Lytton. Timothy Spears. Barry Bayley. Edward Lytton. Timothy Spears. Barry Bayley. Timothy Spears Spears Spears Spears…

They hold no significance for me. They are just words, just letters, just finger movements, just clicking and clacking, just the root cause of my carpal tunnel syndrome not to mention my nightmares. Typing makes my wrists hurt. Sitting at my desk makes my back hurt. Blood does not flow through my body very well. I am just sitting here most of the time, just rotting away and typing, typing, typing.

I often dream of those names and of sinister forms I am compelled to fill out. I am haunted by the monotony night after night. Those names have been burned into my brain but, like I said, they are no longer names. They are structures. They are skyscrapers in my brain. They are towers reaching up to poke holes in the sky. They are temples rattling back and forth.

Someone is calling my name.

I don't know what they want and I don't care. Can't they just leave me alone while I work? Is that too much to ask in this day and age? I guess they are so used to being distracted by things that they don't have any respect for someone who is able to focus on their work.

More noise. The floor is rumbling. Something is creaking and groaning. I don't want to look around because that will just make me part of the environment and I don't want to be part of it even as an observer. When I become an observer, I also become the observed. If I look, then I will be looked *at*. I don't like that. I don't like that at all.

Please, won't they just let me sit in my box undisturbed?

More noise. Things are falling off my desk now. It is too loud in here. What's happening? Why am I being disturbed?

More things are falling off my desk.

More dust is falling from the ceiling. Most screams and shouts. More alarms going off. More confusion. Thanks to my medication, I'm not cowering underneath my desk. Thanks to my medication, I'm not slashing my chest and stomach with the nearest sharp object. Thanks to my medication, I no longer consider myself a martyr.

So now what?

All my coworkers are on the ground now. They are so lazy. They aren't doing any work. I guess I'll just sit here and continue to type, type, type, type, type.

XXXII. NEWLY SHAVEN

Eddie doesn't know much but he knows he's been set up. Yes, he knows that much. For some people, that's *too* much for him to know. He shouldn't know anything. He should barely know his name. He should only be able to babble semi-coherent sentences.

But Eddie knows.

This is what he knows:

On Monday night his cell phone rang and it was the guy Eddie had met at the strip club, the guy who said he had a job available if Eddie didn't mind construction and demolition. Of course, yes, that would be great. Eddie had given the guy his number and told him he'd be waiting for the call.

So on Monday night the phone rang and it was the guy. Eddie wasn't surprised that he had called but he *was* surprised at how much his voice had changed. It didn't even sound like the same guy.

The voice told Eddie where to go on Tuesday morning. Short notice, yes, but that was unavoidable. Eddie said he'd be there, no problem.

And now Eddie knows it was a set up. He knows it probably wasn't the same guy's voice on the phone and that's why Eddie was now locked inside a storage closet on the second floor of an office building in an industrial park.

It smells like disinfectant and mint urinal cakes.

Eddie idly tries the doorknob again but it doesn't budge. The lock must be the best on the market. He kicks the door. It feels like a several inches of steel though Eddie doubts that is possible.

It is a shame that he is stuck in here simply because he had chosen to go to a strip club instead of the usual bar he frequents. He made small talk with the man sitting next to him. If only he had kept his mouth shut and minded his own business. But Eddie has always been friendly and now he is paying for it.

He yells for help.

He knows no one can hear him. The closet seems impenetrable. He can hear no sound through the walls or the door. He is sure no sound can leave the room. Still, he yells again. He yells and yells.

His cell phone rings.

Eddie looks at it and doesn't recognize the phone number. He lets it ring a few more times and then answers it.

"Hello?"

"Ed, hey," the voice says. "It's Tim."

"Who?"

"Tim."

"Tim who?"

"Just listen, man," the voice says. "In a few minutes, the entire building is coming down."

"What? What are you talking about?"

"Just be quiet for a second. The building you're in. It's coming down. They decided to pull it. You have ten maybe fifteen minutes, tops. I wish I had some better news for you but that's it."

Eddie grimaces at the phone. "How do I get out of here?"

"I don't know, man. This wasn't my department. I'm just trying to be a nice guy and let you know."

"What? I don't understand. "

"Maybe you don't need to, I don't know. But you seriously have, like, ten minutes now so call who you have to call or pray or something. Just don't spend the last few minutes talking to *me*."

Eddie mutters something into the phone. Even he does not know what the words mean. He smashes the cell phone on the cement floor.

XXXIII. UNIVERSE DAZE

I am walking through the city and I am stabbed.

I am not stabbed with a knife. I am stabbed with something much smaller. In fact, it feels more like a pinch than a stab. I am minding my own business, keeping to myself, keeping my head down as to not make eye contact with anyone and I feel a sharp pain in my lower back.

It hurts.

And it's burning.

I look around me and see shocked faces of fellow pedestrians. Someone shouts and then another person shouts and before I know it, my ears hurt from all the noise. I hear every car horn and conversation around me. I want everyone to shut up. I want everything to stop making noise.

It feels like there might be blood dripping down my lower back and into my pants. I don't want to touch it just in case I damage the wound in some way. I can't stand the sight of my own blood. I think that's an instinctual thing. It reminds me of my mortality. I don't want to die. Most of the time, I live under the impression that I will *never* die. So I ignore this wound. Maybe if I just pretend it's not there, it will cease to exist. My mortality will cease to exist.

It still hurts, though. It burns and there are people still screaming. Some of the people are touching me now. They tell me to sit down. They tell me to calm down even though I think I am calmer than they are. They are going to get help but I don't need help. If I needed anything, I'd say I just need to get away from all this noise. Everyone and everything is annoying me.

I have to get out of here.

Someone is pushing me down now. They are pulling up the back of my suit jacket. I'm trying to push them away but my arms are too heavy. My legs won't support my weight and the people push me down easily.

It's getting really noisy now. It's pretty crowded, too. From this perspective I see car tires and exhaust. It's bumper to bumper traffic out here. I see shoes and ankles. I see flakes of garbage and debris flying by. I hear the roar of a loud engine. It's not a car engine. It's not a bus. I think we all know what it is.

It's the end of our work day as we know it. It's the end of how we walk down the street to go to work or to the store. It's the end of how we approach danger. Of course, we are all in danger now. At every second of every day we are in complete and utter danger. Everything is dangerous at all times.

The roar in the sky makes my wound throb. It's all coming down now. I don't think it's a surprise and everyone else with half a brain probably isn't surprised either. The sound is terrifying but magnificent. It sounds like I imagine angels would sound if they came down from the heavens to blow their horns or ride their chariots. It's an aural rush, an awakening. I am still terrified, though. And my wound is bleeding out.

And it's coming for me. No one else around me knows it but I do. I guess I'm going to have to go with the flow. It's not like I have a choice. No one really has a choice.

Despite the crowd being in my way, I see it. I see everything.

It hurts.

And it's burning.

XXXIV. BAD LIGHTING

Ronald goes back to his house where he finds his wife locked in the basement.

"Honey?"

There is no answer. He hears sounds of movement in the room, however. He knocks on the door. "Hon? Open the door, please."

No answer. Just noise.

"I'm going to call the doctor, okay? I just want you to talk to him about what's going on. I just want what's best for you, okay? Please, just open the door."

Silence.

The door opens.

Susan stands in the doorway in her bra and underwear. She is covered in dust and grime. "What?" she says.

"Honey, let's just call the doctor. He wants to talk to you."

"About what, Ron?"

"About everything. You can't deny there's a problem here."

"Where, Ron? Where is there a problem? With *me*? *Me*?"

"I didn't say that, Susan. I just think there are some problems and we need help."

"You mean I need help, Ron."

"Come on, hon."

"The only problem I see is that you won't believe anything I say. You think I'm crazy. Do the guys at work even know you're married? Or maybe you tell them you're married to a nutcase. Do you tell them that, Ron? Do you tell them your wife is insane?"

"Of course not, Susan. Stop being ridiculous."

"I'm not being ridiculous and you know it. You're just afraid. Afraid of what people will think of you if you don't blend in."

"I'm getting the phone and then we're going to call the doctor."

"I don't want to. What the hell is he going to say to me? He's just going to try to prescribe me more meds or get me locked up somewhere."

"Susan…"

"That's it, isn't it? You two talked about having me locked away. Is that it, Ron? Is that it?"

"No, will you just come on and let me call the doctor."

"Get out of here!" she screams and shuts the door in her husband's face.

Ronald grunts and pushes the door open. He rushes into the room and grabs his wife.

She screams. "Stop! You're going to rape me, aren't you? You're going to rape me!"

"What's the matter with you, Susan? Jesus Christ! I'm not going to hurt you. Will you just calm down?"

They struggle and Ronald loosens his grip. He does not want his wife to get hurt again. He lets her get out of his grasp.

She yells. "Death squads, Ron!"

"Susan, Jesus, there are *no* death squads."

"Open your eyes, Ron! They're everywhere. They're called by different names but they're everywhere. Cops, security guards, mercenaries, even missionaries. Most of them are in death squads!"

"Jesus Christ, Susan. Come on. Stop with that."

"Even Mother Teresa. Even Mother Teresa was part of a death squad. She was in charge of one."

"Stop being ridiculous."

Susan gritted her teeth. "It's *true*, Ron. She killed people with AIDS."

"That's a horrible thing to say, Susan. Christ…"

"Sometimes the truth is horrible."

"I'm calling the doctor and you're talking to him. If you don't…"

"What, Ron? What are you going to do if I don't talk to the doctor? What? Tell me. Tell me what you're going to do? Are you going to lock me up in a nuthouse?"

"Susan, stop."

"You're going to lock me up in a nuthouse where I'll be raped. That's what's going to happen, Ron. Do you know that? They are going to rape me. They are going to give me meds to knock me out and then they are going to violate me. How do you feel about that? You feel good trying to get me locked up, Ron?"

"Jesus Christ, Susan."

"Do you have any idea what the doctors are going to do to me? They have deals with the military to experiment on people like me! And you don't care. You don't care. You're trying to get rid of me."

"Susan, enough!"

"Death squads!"

XXXV. OF MILK AND SAND

We soaked the tyrants in their own blood and in the blood of their children. We do not regret this. We have no guilt. We have no remorse. We will do it a million more times if we have to. We will repeat our actions until the tyranny is demolished. We will prevail despite our handicaps and our pain.

Our acts are acts of freedom. Our rhetoric and propaganda are expressions of a liberty-minded people. Our violence is a demonstration of a love for both humanity and for YOU KNOW WHO.

We have seen our own loved ones dissolve in the sand, their faces sunburned and gasping for air. We have seen them bleed from every pore, chemicals turning them into mere puppets of battle. We have memorized their last words. We have tattooed them on our skin. We have seen everything and we do not forget. We will never forget. Never forget.

We will continue to soak the tyrants in their own waste. We will turn their cities into mausoleums and transform the sky above their heads into a firmament of smoke and debris. The only heaven these tyrants will know will be the heaven we create for them out of glass, concrete, and steel.

Do you hear our prayers? We never cease to pray. Even in slumber and pain and in death, we pray. Even as we choke on our own poison gas, we pray.

Do you hear our cheers as we watch the tyrants and their brood burning alive in their caves? You can hear our voices on the wind as it blows through our cities. You can record our voices. You can play them back. You can send them to the press. You can broadcast them wherever and whenever you want. The entire world will know our lament.

The entire world will know how we struck the tyrants and brought them to their knees. They will know we regret nothing. We will do it again and again and again. We will strike fear into their familiar places. We will deprive them of sleep and of comfort. We will even bring their tiniest children to revolt against them. We will be the executioners they've only read about in books.

Our acts are justified. Our acts are our livelihood. Our acts are acts of freedom. Never forget that. Never forget.

XXXVI. TWO MINARETS

Bunting smashes the videotapes.

Hundreds of hours of footage are being destroyed. But Bunting is not angry. He is perfectly calm as he smashes years of preparation. He has watched each tape dozens of times and has memorized the footage. The tapes are unnecessary. They are redundant. He has all the footage in his mind.

The preparation has brought him to this, the few moments before his mission is to begin. He is ready. Or rather, he is as ready as he will ever be. He knows no one can really be ready for this sort of thing. Man was not designed for this. It takes a special man to even consider this mission.

He smashes more tapes.

The office he's in is on the top floor of a three-story building in an industrial park. The lease has one of Bunting's names on it. He doesn't remember which one but that's okay. He won't need to renew the lease.

He smashes more tapes.

He thinks about his birth.

Though Bunting was born a British citizen, he never felt allegiance to that country or its people. He doesn't hate or despise them. He is simply apathetic. The royal family does nothing for him either, does not hold his heart in patriotic rapture. They are simply people on display. That is all. He has fantasized many times about raping the queen. The fantasy wasn't out of any sexual desire but rather the desire to desecrate the royal family, to turn the figurehead into receptacle for his excretions. He fantasized about filming the violation as well. He wanted to record *everything*.

Growing up, Bunting was fascinated by the media coverage of the royals despite his distaste for them. He was fascinated not by the people themselves but by how the cameras captured them. The cameramen were gods or, at least, the messengers of gods. At a very young age, Bunting started recording media reports off the television. He studied the camerawork, studied the people displayed on the news. He took it all in and regurgitated it into his own video work.

Bunting thinks about his childhood.

He smashes more videotapes.

He realizes he could have spent his time better. Yes, he finds solace in the obsessions. Yes, he feels comfortable in his cocoon of video footage. But he knows this safe haven is not permanent. It is all leading up to one ultimate act of filming, one cataclysmic act that will awaken Bunting's conscience to a freedom he has never experienced before.

He is no longer behind the camera. Bunting is in front of the camera, the camera that is invisible to the eye but always present. He is performing for the masses who are watching him on their televisions.

He is the last great actor in the greatest act in history.

XXXVII. NEARING ZERO

Tina is being prepped for surgery.

"You okay?" the nurse asks.

"I guess so."

"Nothing to be worried about. It will be fine."

"I know," Tina says but does not know if she believes it. She had felt strange walking into the surgery center and seeing she was the only patient. There were no other people except for the nurse and the two doctors.

"Any questions before the doctors come in?" the nurse asks.

"How long will this take? I don't remember what Dr. Corbelli said."

The nurse smiles. "As long as it takes." She leaves the room and shuts the door.

Tina is left on the operating table, left alone to listen to the hum of the small refrigerator in the corner of the room.

She hears loud sounds from the waiting room. She wonders if something is wrong. She does not want to delay the operation any longer. Tina leans on her elbows and calls out.

"Hello?"

There is no answer.

She leans back and stares at the ceiling where there are cracks that resemble rivers on a filthy map. Tina sees more cracks forming. She feels the hum of the refrigerator grow louder.

She leans up again and says, "Hello?"

There is no answer.

XXXVIII. ENJINEERS

We read books written by dust devils and published by jinn. We study every word, memorize every syllable. Our business thrives on the beautiful cadence of the paragraphs. Our offices are illuminated by their rhythm.

Yet we feel empty.

We long for our brains to gather sand. We long for heavy heads and hearts to weigh us down in the oceanic ruins. We long for profits.

All profits lead to the demolished men. They are reconstructed into automobiles and driven through foreign lands. Our books recount their legacy through the guttural language of the devils. But the demolished men are less than satisfied with their rebirth.

If only we could fill ourselves with some sort of divine heat, some fiery pronunciation of primitive holy words. Then, perhaps, we could find the authors of our books and watch them construct financial sigils.

Our deconstructive hand devices will illuminate the path. Two blank eyes stare at us and burn. We put out their fires with frivolous paperwork. We will not be filing those reports. We are sorry for the inconvenience.

We used to worship the demolished men. We used to worship their corruption and their infidelity. We used to bathe in their rivers and worship at their gargantuan temples. We did all of this to appease the imposters. They were not real devils! They were not real jinn! They were smokeless adversaries hidden under robes and guns.

But we prospered.

And now our business thrives.

We climb all those towers in all those hells and savor every moment of our meditative hallucinations. We treasure every second we count down to annihilation. We are no longer fathers or mothers, brothers or sisters, sons or daughters. We are the collective business of extermination and retaliation. We are righteousness and freedom, intelligence and honor.

We will lead you. You may follow us.

Our deconstructive hand devices will illuminate the path. You may follow us. We will not be filing those reports. We are sorry for the inconvenience.

You may follow us.

XXXIX. THE ENJINEER

Dr. Corbelli watches the nurse walk out of the operating room and over to her desk. He admires her large chest, the breasts that seem to hang down almost to her waist. Yes, for an older woman, she is very desirable. Corbelli feels his blood pressure rise. His body is reacting to thoughts of the nurse revealing her breasts to him, calling to him to feed on her milk. Corbelli was never breastfed as a child and he finds the concept exhilarating and taboo. He wonders how much each breast must weigh. They are huge. They are massive. They are distracting.

He walks over to the nurse. "Is our patient ready?"

"She's ready, doctor."

Corbelli moves his face close to the nurse's. "Are *you* ready?"

"Yes, I'm ready."

Corbelli grabs at her chest, feels her gigantic breasts

within his grip.

The nurse shouts. "Doctor!"

"You said you were ready."

"Please! No!"

"You're ready for intercourse. I can feel it. Your body is ready for the incision."

"Doctor!"

Corbelli proceeds with the rape. He penetrates the nurse and stifles her cries with his hand. When he finishes, he digs into his pocket, takes out a pill, and sticks it into the nurse's mouth. "Swallow it."

She whimpers but complies.

Corbelli says, "Now please let Dr. Sotos know I'm ready."

XL. BLACK SEPTEMBER

The throne does not move.

On this throne, let us imagine there sits God, this supernatural being who is most likely a deranged sadist. We can imagine a drooling hunchback who spends its eternal days masturbating and drawing blood with its mangled teeth. This God watches us from his throne, and destroys us, sends its malevolent thoughts into the world for its amusement and our punishment. This God's thoughts consist mainly of decayed babble. This mentally-retarded hunchback of heaven gets particular pleasure out of demolishing its own creations as well the creations of its creations. This hunchback's heavenly drool falls from the sky in the form of hurricanes. It lets loose dandruff in the form of disease.

This is what I think about on my flight to Los Angeles.

This is what I dream about while on my way to the

commune.

I also dream of silence. I do not want to hear the roar of the engines or the shouting of the noisy people who are trying their best to keep me awake. No, I do not want to hear the screams. I want silence.

There is a roar that frightens me. It turns into a rumbling. It fills my ear with dust.

For a second I believe it is God finally moving his throne across the firmament. He is scraping the floor of his throne room. He is *destroying* the floor. He is giving up on us.

A voice over the intercom says, "Will passenger Tim Osman Spears please come to the cockpit? Will Tim Osman Spears please come to the cockpit?"

A different voice from behind me asks, "You related to Billy Spears?"

I say, "No."

"Are you sure?"

"Yes."

"Did you ever work at the post office?"

"No."

"Hey, is that cocaine?"

"No."

"What is it?"

I don't answer. I just want silence. I don't know why I answered in the first place.

The intercom again says, "Tim Osman Spears *please* come to the cockpit."

What now? I do not want to go to the cockpit. There

is too much commotion up there. I can see a struggle. I can see a noisy situation I do not want to get involved in.

I can hear the throne move again. It is moving into my silence. The dust fills my ears. I look out the window.

I get up from my seat and walk to the cockpit.

XLI. TAKFIR AL-FIRTAK

Barry wakes up on his couch.

As his eyes open, his wife walks through the front door. She looks surprised to see him. Her hair is messy and her lipstick is smeared. She is out of breath.

"Barry, you're home," she says. She sounds disappointed.

"Uh, yeah…" Barry says, wiping his face and trying to remember how he ended up on the couch. He never falls asleep here.

The word SECURITY pops into his mind.

"Why aren't you at work?" she says.

"I don't know," Barry says.

"Well, I was just stopping home for a minute. I'm going back out. I'll be a little late, though. Are you okay on your own for dinner?"

Barry tries to get up off the couch but fails. "Yeah, sure, whatever."

"Okay," his wife says, walking in the bathroom quickly.

Barry leans his head back and thinks about his wife having sex with another man.

XLII. CAMEL AND BUSINESS PARK

In the haze of surgery, Tina is handed a cell phone. A voice whispers in her ear, "Call your parents."

Tina doesn't feel herself dial the numbers but she watches her fingers as they do so. The phone is at her ear.

"Hello?" her mother answers.

Tina doesn't speak. A voice whispers in her other ear, "Say hello to Mommy."

Tina speaks. "Mom…"

"Tina?"

"Mom…"

"Tina? Is that you? What's the matter?"

"I'm getting better…"

"What are you talking about? Where are you?"

"Doctors…"

"Doctors?"

"Doctors…"

"What doctors?"

A voice whispers in Tina's other ear, "Tell Mommy you saw the minarets."

"Mommy…" Tina says.

The voice again, "Tell her!"

"Mommy…I saw…the minarets…"

"Tina, what are you talking about? Wait, I'm going to put your dad on the phone. Hold on."

The other voice whispers, "Don't speak to Daddy!"

The cell phone is taken away and smashed against the wall. Tina feels a needle enter the back of her neck and sleep comes fast and so does the pain.

XLIII. WHITE PLANES

You are done with your research.

All planning is done. All tests are done. All experiments are done. Everything is complete. All that's next is the reality of things, the acts themselves, the extension of your thought into actuality.

You have planned your "acts of terror" but you know you may be the only one left terrified. You are the only one who truly understands your intent. You are the only one who fully grasps the lengths you have had to go and the risks you've had to take. It is all very frightening indeed.

Your cell phone rings.

You answer it and listen to the voice asking if you are ready. You are annoyed at the implication that you might *not* be ready. You are always ready. You are ready right now. You are done with your research. All planning is done. All tests are done. All experiments are done.

Everything is complete and you are ready.

You tell them you are ready. They grunt and end the call. You are left holding a dead cell phone. You want to call your father but know he will not speak to you. That is upsetting. If there was any moment that was necessary for a father and son relationship, it was *this* moment. You need this moment to be filled with your father's voice.

He won't speak to you but you contemplate calling him anyway. You may just hear his voice for a few seconds. You may just hear him saying, "Hello? Hello?" That is all you really want, isn't it? You only need that small sound to comfort you, something to fill the silent void now that your research is done.

You dial his number.

You let it ring.

You want him to answer in a good mood. You want him to answer in a way that tells you that he will be receptive to your call. You know that is not going to be the case. He will answer with a gruff voice. He will not greet you as a son.

A voice answers. "Hello?"

You say, "Dad, it's me."

There is no reply so you again say, "Dad, it's me."

"I heard you."

"It's me, Dad…"

"Yeah."

"I wanted to call you."

"I have nothing to say to you."

"I'm not sick anymore."

"What?"

"I'm not sick anymore. The medicine is helping."

"You'll always be sick. Don't call me again."

"But I love you…"

Your dad sighs heavily into the phone and then ends the call, leaving you with a pain in your chest and an image of your father towering over you, grimacing, lecturing, and pointing his finger in your face.

You smash the cell phone on the cement floor.

You cry.

XLIV. HUNGER

Barry tells the pharmacist his name and that he should have a prescription waiting for him.

"Sorry, sir," the pharmacist says. "That specific medicine has been discontinued."

"What?"

"The medication Taborica is no longer available. Unfortunately there is no generic for it so you'll have to go to you physician to get something else."

Barry frowns. "Are you kidding me?"

"No."

The pharmacist leans in close and whispers. "If it makes you feel any better, I heard that Taborica was just a placebo anyway."

"That's impossible."

"Nothing's impossible with medicine."

XLV. FLIGHTS

"And what were they prescribed when they came back?"

"Taborica, sir."

"Taborica?"

"Yes, sir."

"What is that?"

"The papers are right in front of you, sir."

"Oh, yes. Thank you."

"You're welcome, sir."

"So we think it was this Taborica that caused the... incidents?"

"That's what I've been told, sir. There's no way to know for sure."

"Goddamn astronauts."

"Not just the astronauts, sir. The men on the ground as well."

"What?"

"Yes, the men in the launch control room were affected as well."

"Jesus *Christ*."

"I told their families we would pray for them."

"Why'd you go and do a thing like that?"

"I was simply being polite, sir."

"Well, next time you should know better. Politeness never solved any problems or won any wars. What we need is more research. Get me some of this Taborica."

"It's been recalled, sir."

"Recalled?"

"Yes, sir."

"Well, get me some. I don't care how you do it."

"Yes, sir."

"I want to experience what these men have experienced."

"Very good, sir."

"You, too."

"Pardon?"

"I want you to experience the same. You and I will take this Taborica. We will take it together."

"I don't know how I feel about that, sir."

"I don't care *how* you feel about it."

"Okay, sir. But this seems like a dangerous thing to do."

"We're men. This is what men *do*."

XLVI. FRIEDRICER

Tim rides the Tokyo subway while dressed as a clown. He is holding balloons. He is glad no one has laughed at him yet.

He scratches his face and looks at the greasepaint on his finger and underneath his fingernail. He regrets dressing up as a clown. He does not regret bringing the balloons, though. They are necessary.

Tim bends over and picks up the umbrella that is underneath his seat. A man standing next to him shakes his head.

Tim knows this is the signal. He pulls out a tape recorder from underneath the seat and presses RECORD. He pops one of the balloons with the sharp tip of the umbrella. A cell phone goes off, the ring tone is the theme song to a popular children's show from the 1970s. Tim pops another balloon.

There is chaos around the clown.

The ring tone plays on and on as people shout and start to fall, clutching their throats. Tim wipes more greasepaint off his face and lets the rest of the balloons float to the ceiling.

People don't notice the clown running through the subway car. Tim finds this amusing. More cell phones go off and more theme songs fill the air. Tim waves his cassette recorder in the air and then holds it up to a woman who is coughing and choking. Tim knows the cassette will make for good listening later once it goes through the editing process.

Tim moves the cassette recorder to another person, a man who is banging on the subway car door, trying to get out. The man is crying. Drool is dripping off his chin.

Tim backs away from the man and blows into the microphone of the recorder. A hand falls on his shoulder. A voice says, "I think we're done here."

Tim looks back and meets eyes with a man who looks oddly like his father.

XLVII. PURE

Tina's eyes flutter. She is awake from surgery. She is alone.

She looks at her crotch but sees only fog. In her peripheral vision she sees small shapes scurrying along the walls. She ignores them.

Trying to move her arms, Tina fails. They are too heavy. She moves her legs, though, and drops them over the sides of the operating table. She slowly gets off and starts to walk.

The room is empty. There is no sound but the refrigerator. It is not a comforting sound.

She looks down at herself again but the fog is still there. If she had use of her hands she would put them into the fog.

Tina walks out of the room, her arms dead at her sides. She walks and walks and walks. She is not expecting to see anyone else but she wishes someone was there. She has many questions to ask.

"Hello?"

She walks and walks and finds herself at the end of a white hallway. In fact, she notices that everything is white. Is that odd for a medical center? She doesn't think so. White is a sterile color. It is a pure color. Is it a color at all?

The door at the end of the hallway is taller than all the other doors. Tina doesn't know how she will get in without use of her hand. But then her hands move. They are no longer dead things. They are hers once again.

She opens the door and walks into the room. It is really that simple. The room is filled with mirrors and one small light.

Nude and curious, Tina stands in the middle of the room. She is a newly born beast in a wilderness of mirrors. She looks at her images in the mirrors and sees that the fog has lifted.

Her crotch is unveiled.

It is not a penis, not two penises. It is not a vagina. It is something else entirely. It brings tears to Tina's eyes and laughter to her throat. Her knees weaken. She wants to drop to the floor and worship her images but she knows her image will follow her to the ground, making worship impossible.

Her arms move. She stretches them out and brings them to her crotch. Her fingers are engulfed in the surgical-born splendor that has replaced the previous incarnation of her genitals.

Tina wants to find a phone. She wants to find a phone and call her parents. She wants to explain everything to them, tell them that she is not sorry for her decision, that she is not a freak, not an embarrassment. She is…what is she? Tina doesn't know exactly. That doesn't matter, though. What matters is that the surgery was successful.

She walks closer to one of the mirrors and kisses her reflection.

It is her first real kiss.

XLVIII. ECCLESIASTES 1:18

It's been a while since I've been in a city. I have no plans to go ever again much to my wife's dismay. For me, the desire to go into the city has always been overshadowed by my fear of tall structures.

I've been to the city before, yes, so I know what I'm talking about. It was on those occasions that I've been terrified by those massive monstrosities of steel and glass that surrounded me. It seems so unnatural that people would build structures that tall. The very height of those buildings is enough to make a person dizzy and struck with a feeling of insignificance. That is why I no longer go into the city.

Humans are animals that have stepped over their bounds, have charged their way into a territory they have no business being in. They have constructed one Tower of Babel after another and I have to suffer for it. I have to feel persecuted by feelings of fearful irrelevance whenever gazing at such a structure. I don't deserve to feel that way. I don't deserve to feel as if the buildings may topple on top of me at any moment. Communities are necessary but sky high cities are crimes against nature, against the natural order of things. It is an abuse of architectural evolution. What's next? What other obscenity will come about from our desire to conquer and inhabit empty space?

But it isn't just the buildings that have made me swear off trips to the city. It is the noise as well. It is not just the sound of traffic and a thousand people talking at the same time that repulses me. There is an underlying *hum* of the city. I don't know if anyone else hears it or if they hear it the same way I do. I imagine people living in the city may very well have grown used to the hum and no longer actually hear it except on a subliminal level. I cannot fault them for that. However, I found the sound unbearable once I noticed it. It sickens me. It makes me feel like I'm dissolving, that I'm becoming less of a human being from the simple act of *hearing* it.

My wife puts her arm around me and says, "Let's go into the city and see a show."

"No," I say.

"It'll be good for you to get out of the house."

"No, it won't."

"Come on. We haven't gone out in months. I don't feel like being cooped up in the house all the time. It'll be good for you."

"No."

"Come on…"

"It won't be good for me at all."

XLIX. MORE STRUCTURES

Someone has left a bunch of Xeroxed pictures around the apartment.

I walk out of the bathroom and see them scattered on the floor and crudely taped to the walls. The pictures are all the same: a grainy black-and-white reproduction of an architectural blueprint. It looks complex, something I will never have a chance of really understanding though it is something I would study as if the complexity itself would make me more intelligent.

Everyone in the apartment is at the window, their noses mashed up on the glass, looking out at something with their eyes all wide and their mouths gaping. What the hell are they looking at? I'm always late to things. I always miss out. For once I'd like to be included in something. Why didn't someone come get me? Was I in the bathroom that long?

I don't want to continue to be the odd man out so

I join them. That's all I need: for someone to make a comment about me, about my not wanting to be part of the family.

With my nose mashed up against the warm glass, I look out the window. Now I know why someone left those Xeroxed pictures around the apartment. And I thank them for it.

L. SONOCYTOLOGIST

Barry puts the cassette into his stereo and presses PLAY. The sounds come out in a deluge. The speakers shake and after only a few seconds, they implode. They are destroyed by the noise.

Barry kicks the speakers repeatedly. There is still some sound coming out of them, a horrible low sound like the roar of a tsunami or the manipulated sounds of a jet engine. He hates the sound. It reminds him of the ocean.

A voice is buried underneath the sound. It says, "Happy enjoy happiness." Then there are more voices in multiple languages but Barry doesn't know what they're saying. He can only imagine. He translates them falsely in his mind.

"Happy things and buildings."

"Black mosque machinery database."

"We could probably substitute a generic brand but it

might not work as well."

"Blacked out for a minute."

"Works just fine."

"I feel something."

"Change transfer complex."

"Pull it."

"Prions or something."

"Probably nothing."

"I'd like to make an appointment."

"Blacked out for a second."

"Do you have an appointment?"

"Yes, works just fine."

"No, I don't. Is that a problem?"

"No one has read the roadside announcements."

"Never forget you are invited."

"Swissair 1970. Reggio 1970. Banco De Vizcaya 1983."

"What kind of surgery?"

"And yes, I wash my hands before I leave."

"Because is the fall of…"

Barry does not mind that all the translations are false. He decides all human perception consists of inaccurate interpretations and translations of someone else's expression. He also realizes he is going through Taborica withdrawal.

He looks at the ruins of the speakers and wonders what his wife will say. Will she even care? Will she overlook it because she knows he is going through tough times? Will she overlook it because she is having sex with another man?

Barry puts his hand in his pants and starts looking for lumps in his scrotum. He doesn't want to find any but he slowly massages the region and thinks about things unrelated to his genitals. He closes his eyes and thinks about flying.

He finds a lump.

He opens his eyes and thinks about crashing.

LI. ZONING BOARD

Voices. Silence. Tape hiss. A high pitched whistling. Hands clapping. Cheers. A muffled voice says, "Boom." Silence. Tape hiss. A low rumble. Voices. Metallic clanging. Squealing. A muffled voice says, "Pull it." Cheers. Glass breaking. Fire crackling. Cheers. Silence. Tape hiss. A low rumble. Door slamming. Car engine. Cheers. High pitched feedback. Tires screeching. Hands clapping. Silence. Tape hiss. Hum of a fluorescent light bulb. A loud voice says, "Pull it." Silence. Tape hiss. A digitalized voice says, "What is your emergency?"

There is the low end sound, the pit-of-your-stomach sound that rumbles, rumbles, rumbles until you think about taking the cassette and smashing it against the cement floor of your garage. It is a document of some tragedy in the outer dark. It is not real for you but it is making you nauseous nonetheless. It is causing you to feel for something that isn't exactly real or at least not real *to you*. After all, you weren't there.

You've heard the recording dozens of times. You have written stories about the sounds. You have drawn pictures of the sounds. You have even made recordings of your own: pale imitations of what you have heard on the recording. You made several copies of your own recordings that you sent to local reporters and to independent music magazines. You do not know what else to do but be sick and cautious of anyone who finds the smallest interest in your work. You do not care what the reporters say or what the reviewers say. You did not send it to them for reassurance. You do not care what they have to say. What you do want is for them to say something about the recording *to other people*. You want the knowledge of your recordings to spread like a virus.

However, you would not be able to deal with anyone else who listens to this cassette. You know what type of person that would be. You know that anyone who enjoys these sounds is waiting to venture into that outer dark and you don't want to be there. The low rumbling sound like the earth groaning, that sound that reminds you of drowning, of being smothered by tons of cement and steel, that is the sound that makes you ill and keeps you away from all structures. You hide in your basement with powdered milk and comic books. You fill journal after journal with deconstructions of your dreams. You do not interpret them. You want to make that clear. You do *not* interpret them. You simply deconstruct them into their most basic parts and try to fit them into any current political situation you can find on the news channels on the small television you keep on the basement floor. You do not read newspapers. Newspapers are slow journeys to the past. Newspaper articles are not manipulated enough. Also, the newspapers themselves can easily be poisoned. It is easy to put poison into ink. Anyway, you want to see people on the television move, talk, and manipulate their surroundings until the news is just like the dreams you have deconstructed. Your dreams are rather banal. They are not fantastical in the least. They are simply extensions of your daily life or rather, what your daily life used to be. You often dream of supermarkets. You dream about walking down the aisles and shopping for snacks. You have a lot of dreams about shopping. You wonder if your subconscious is trapped in some sort of capitalistic bubble. You don't mind. You see the beauty of this dreamlike capitalism. You enjoy money and you enjoy the dreams it brings. You dream you are shopping at a comic store and buying comics you passed up when you were a child. You dream of being in an accident in front of a shopping mall. You dream of meeting a pale, pedophiliac version of Stan Laurel.

There are explosions but no one is hurt. You wake up relieved.

The first side of the cassette is over but you are reluctant to turn it over. What sort of sounds will reveal themselves in the last forty-five minutes? You can only imagine it will be more deconstructions of world events.

YOUR CITIES YOUR TOMBS

You imagine silence, tape hiss, silence, tape hiss, silence, tape hiss, rumbling, roaring, explosions, explosions, explosions, shouting, glass breaking, silence, tape hiss, clicking, car doors slamming, voices, silence.

You do not understand the order of things but you realize you don't need to understand or even attempt to understand. Being in the vicinity of such an order is enough for you to get the benefits of fate. And what is your fate?

You will simply cease to exist without knowing why or how. That's it.

Silence. Tape hiss.

You will simply cease to exist.

Silence.

LII. PARKLAND HOSPITAL, BEIRUT

Tina walks out of the surgery center and finds herself in the middle of an industrial park.

It is evening. There are no people, cars, or trucks. Everything is silent. Tina stumbles onto the asphalt and looks around. She sees a sign that says BUTTO BUT-TO CORPORATION and another that says RAMS HORNS VIDTECH INTERNATIONAL. The names sound familiar.

Tina is naked.

She is comfortable with this. For the first time in her life, she is secure in her nudity. She is confident and proud. The mirrors have made her this way. They have guaranteed her freedom from the past.

Tina walks down the street which consists only of asphalt and large buildings used for manufacturing and distribution. It is peaceful. Tina enjoys it. She also enjoys the feel of the asphalt on her feet. It is slightly spongelike. She bounces her heels and enjoys the sensation.

She sees a dumpster and approaches it. Inside there is large pile of garbage. Tina pulls herself up and jumps inside the dumpster. On top of the pile are burnt vinyl records. *Gris-Gris* by Dr. John, *Pretzel Logic* by Steely Dan, *Hannover Interruption* by Merzbow, *Be My Twin* by Brother Beyond, *New York* by Lee Towers. Underneath the records are dozens of broken model airplanes, Halloween masks, plastic tubing, comic books, pill bottles, syringes, green and white scarves, cigarettes, and several notebooks.

Tina digs through and pulls out a pill bottle. She opens it and sees there are three pills left. She pours them into her mouth and chews on them, filling her mouth with a bitter chemical taste. The pill dust is absorbed on and under her tongue.

Euphoria runs through Tina's body. There are planes overhead leaving thick trails of white smoke. She hears a man outside the dumpster. He might be talking on a cell phone because Tina doesn't hear anyone reply.

"Did you hear what I just said?" the voice says. "Press record and pull it."

Tina licks the inside of the pill bottle. She wishes more pills would appear. If only reality worked like that. If only her wishes brought things into existence. She looks at the planes in the sky and worries about the people inside. But *are* there people inside? Tina doesn't know. She can't see them. She doesn't know if they exist. She wonders if they can see her. No, that's ridiculous.

They are too far up to see one person sitting in a dump-ster. She waves. She wants to be seen. She wants to be noticed. She wants to be recognized as someone who has changed for the better. She is not the same as before.

Tina is tempted to climb out of the dumpster to find a phone. She wants to call her parents. She wants to call her cousin. She wants to call the doctors. She wants another operation. She thinks it will be good for her.

The man outside the dumpster is still talking. He sounds agitated now.

Tina wants to take a peek at the man. She wants to put a face to the voice. She wonders if he is a doctor.

"No, absolutely not. You can't back out now, Tim. You can't," the man says.

The sky is now covered by a canopy of white planes. They are getting closer. Tina leans her head back and closes her eyes. She taps her fingers on the dumpster and starts trying to communicate with the man via Morse code.

She sends him a message. "I want out before they come down."

LIII. ZERO MASS RITUAL

It's on television right now.

You see it, don't you?

You see it but you don't believe your eyes.

I see it. I'm recording it on my VCR. I hope a six-hour tape is enough. I hope the quality is good. I hope for a lot of things.

I'm not going to work today. I'm not going to work tomorrow either. Perhaps I'll take the whole week off. I need to restore my mental health. I need to make sure the medication kicks in.

Things happen and we react.

We react to each and every thing. We have no more relationships to destroy now. We are collapsing slowly. We are collapsing in slow-motion. We have been praying for collapse.

Things happen and we overreact.

I print the map out and give you a copy. I've printed

a lot more and I plan on leaving them all around the office once I get back to work. I'll probably leave them around the neighborhood as well. People need to see it. You need to see it. I'd love to know your thoughts about it. Can you see it? Can you read it? Can you tell me what you see? Can you decipher the map?

Things happen.

Do not overreact.

Do you know what to do in the event of an emergency? Tell me about your own emergency procedures. Tell me what you would do in the event of an emergency. Do you have duct tape? Do you have gas masks? Do you have a supply of water? Do you have peanut butter? Do you have saltines? Do you have flashlights? Do you have batteries? Do you have a generator? Do you have canned goods?

I have a corner in the basement all ready. I have blankets and gas masks and canned goods and powdered milk and water jugs and saltines and peanut butter and dried fruit. I have magazines and books and pens and paper and flashlights and batteries and radios. I have a flag, too, that I plan to wave outside once things are safe.

I wish you were here but I know how life works. God's plan is mysterious. Things happen. You know this and I know this.

Things happen.

But I will not overreact.

The medication is kicking in. I can feel it. I'm watching television and I see your face falling from the sky. I'm sorry. I'm very sorry. I wish you had stayed home from work, too. I feel partially responsible for these things.

Things happen.

I hate it.

But these things happen.

This is how life works.

Everything will work out.

Don't overreact.

LIV. PATERS

Barry hears something at the front door. It's the mail-man leaving a package.

But he doesn't remember ordering anything and he's not expecting anyone to send him anything either. He opens the door and picks up the box. The return address is his father's.

His father has sent him a package.

Barry brings it to the kitchen and sets it on the table. He has a seat in front of the box and stares at it. What could be inside? Barry thinks it might be bibles. It might be religious tracts. It might be photo albums. He doesn't know and is afraid to find out.

He is glad his wife isn't home. He doesn't want her to see him so emotionally vulnerable. She's seen enough of that. She's seen him be less than a man more often than he would like.

Barry starts to open the package.

Inside he finds a folded up piece of notebook paper. Under the paper is a pile of photographs. Next to the photographs is a grass-stained baseball. There is also a cassette tape.

He picks up the baseball and looks at the faded signature that has been written on it. Barry has never been a baseball fan despite his father being one. He doesn't know who the signature belongs to because it's faint and illegible.

Barry picks up the note and unfolds it.

LV. THE BUSINESS OF YA'JUJ AND MA'JUJ

I will never get on a plane.

I will never put my life in jeopardy and will never put my life in the figurative hands of an infidel vessel. There is too much danger. We are all in danger at all times.

But I dream of planes.

I dream I am on a flight out of Boston even though I have never been there. I check under my seat and find a plank of wood with a Casio watch duct-taped to it. It is then that I wake up clutching my pillow and feeling as if the bomb has set fire to my bowels. I am alive but sweaty and in fear of danger because we are all in danger at all times.

I will never get on a plane.

I dream I am on a flight to somewhere in Colorado. I check under my seat and find a box full of black gloves and wire. I know I am supposed to do something with the contents but I don't remember what. That's when I wake up on the floor of my bathroom.

I will never get on a plane.

I understand that getting into a car is also dangerous. Because of that, I do not like traveling in cars. They are dangerous machines. I do not trust them. I do not trust the drivers behind the wheel of other cars. I do not even trust myself.

We are in danger, always in danger. We are dangerous beings in a dangerous land. I cannot emphasize this enough. I will keep saying it until the sky burns up in a rainbow of jet fuel and steel. At that point, I will be half a man huddled in my cellar, waiting for the end, waiting for the towers to fall and for the waters to rise to drown the masses.

I am afraid.

I am afraid of the flooding that will come. The waters will rise and I shall be weak from lack of will. I cannot fight the deluge.

Those evil men will escape on their private planes. They will escape the floods and leave the rest of us to drown. They will fly to their private islands. They will leave the rest of us to be tormented by our fears.

I work from home.

The computer allows me to do my work. It allows me to communicate with my coworkers and my superiors. Though I find my job mind-numbing, it allows me to stay in my room and not venture out into the dangerous unknown. I do not leave the house. Everywhere is dangerous. This is why I work from home.

The company I work for is a good one. It is a good company that does good work. It is good for me because it allows me the flexibility to live with the minimum amount of fear. My company understands my fear of danger. For this, I am in their debt. I will do anything for my company. I will do all of my work on time and with no mistakes. I am a dedicated employee.

But I am still afraid.

I am afraid of getting fired. I am afraid of being thought of as weak or incompetent. I am afraid of embarrassment. I am afraid of planes. I am afraid of gossip. I am afraid of confrontations. I am afraid that others will have an inaccurate opinion of me. I am afraid of planes.

Out of my bedroom window I can see several planes crisscross the sky, leaving thick trails of white in their wake. I fear there might be a collision. It is possible. There is danger everywhere including the sky. I watch for a collision. I watch the planes and fear one might crash into my house. For a few seconds I imagine what it would be like to be on a plane at the moments before and during impact. I cannot stop the fear from ruining my body. My stomach hurts now. I cannot stop anything. I am powerless and weak. I am embarrassed. I must get back to work. I am powerless and weak.

I will never get on a plane.

LVI. AND AVES

Barry puts the cassette tape into the stereo and presses PLAY.

His father's voice says, "Okay, it's recording. I think, yeah...okay." There are some noises: someone putting a glass down on a wooden table, a woman's giggle, footsteps. An acoustic guitar starts to play. His father starts to sing.

"On a mission..."

Barry turns the volume up.

"On a mission from the father..."

It doesn't sound like Barry's father, really. He knows it's him, yes, but the voice sounds so different, so alien. It is a younger and more confident version of his father. Barry has never heard it before but knows he is older now than his father was during the recording.

"Spinning rainbows through the night..."

Barry picks up the photographs that accompanied

the cassette. Barry's father as a child, big for his age and looking grumpy. Another one showing his father holding a fishing pole, looking disappointed. Another one of his father as a young adult holding a guitar in front of a tree. His father a few years older, standing in front of a pile of rubble and what looks like the broken foundation of a house. He is surrounded by wire, bricks, metal sheets, and black garbage bags. He is wearing black gloves. The last photograph is of Barry as a child, smiling and being held by his father who is not looking at the camera. His eyes are somewhere far away.

"We're down to zero again…We're down to the heart of it all…again."

Barry puts the photographs down. He closes his eyes.

"I'm trapped in a winner's dream…"

Barry wipes tears off his eyes and presses STOP on the stereo. He goes outside and takes a stick from the ground. He goes back inside his house and rummages through the junk drawers in the kitchen. He puts aside take-out menus, batteries, nails, and finds a small spool of string. He takes a three-foot long piece and cuts it off the spool. He ties it to the stick.

Barry is ready to go fishing.

LVII. IS THEE LION OV JUDAH SLEEPING?

"Police operator 1923, what is your emergency?"

"I'm on the 93rd floor of the Henwich Bingen building. There was just an explosion on one of the floors below us."

"Floor 93 you said?"

"Yes."

"Okay...what's your name?"

"Tim Spears. Tim Osman Spears."

"Spell the last part, please."

"O-s-m-a-n S-p-e-a-r-s."

"Thank you. Now just stay on the line while I put this information in."

"There's smoke now. It's coming in through the doors."

"Smoke?"

"Yeah."

"93rd floor, right?"

"Yeah. You gotta send someone up here. People are starting to leave but I'm not sure if it's safe to go down."

"Just stay where you are, sir."

"Everyone's leaving."

"Just stay where you are. It might not be safe to go down yet. I have Fire on the way."

"They're coming back."

"What did you say, sir? Who's coming back?"

"Everyone's coming back. Wait, hold on…"

"What, sir?"

"They said the stairway is on fire and the elevator's not working."

"Okay, just stay where you are. Someone should be there momentarily."

"It's getting really hard to breathe here."

"Sit tight, okay?"

"Yeah."

"Sir?"

"Ye—.."

"Sir? Are you still there? Sir? Sir?"

LVIII. ACTION, UMM KULTHUM!

Bunting zooms in on the man's face.

He zooms in. He zooms out. He zooms back in for an extreme close-up of the man's pores. They resemble pale craters on the moon. He feels guilty. He has taken this man's wife and made her a harlot. He has penetrated her. He has defiled her.

She had wanted to be validated. She had wanted attention and Bunting had given it to her. She had wanted to feel that she was a hole worth filling and Bunting accomplished that task. He still feels guilty, though, especially when zooming in on her husband's face while the man sleeps.

Bunting is recording the man but plans on smashing the video cassette later. He has no real need to keep it. Once it is recorded, the footage is kept inside Bunting's memory and in the memory of the universe. This is what he believes.

The camera captures everything and brings it into Bunting's brain and into his memory and into his very core. He will not forget the man's face. He will not forget the man's pores, his facial hair. He will not forget the man's impotence.

Bunting wishes it can be different.

But he remembers something now. He remembers the assignment Jali has given him. He is supposed to record the planes and archive the footage. But Bunting has no more tapes. He is using the last one on this man.

What will Jali say?

Bunting does not care.

He is too busy obsessing over this man's impotence and his wife's dissatisfaction. Obsession turns his work into pleasure. It is making his life meaningful. As he records the man's face, he shares the man's destruction. He wonders what the man is dreaming about.

Bunting thinks he knows. He thinks the man is dreaming about the fungal magnificence of buildings, the viral spread of skyscrapers. He is dreaming of automobiles and buses. He dreams of men in basements who swallow secrets too terrible to utter aboveground. The man dreams of atrocities committed by quiet men with razors. He dreams of buildings imploding and exploding. He dreams of dust clouds and crooked planes. He dreams of phone calls.

The man dreams of his virility.

Bunting presses STOP on his video camera.

LIX. PASSENGERS

We sit in silence until noon.

Then we are able to talk and we do just that. We talk about many things. We talk about our dangerous lives or rather, the lives we had before we came here. They were dangerous lives we started to lead and we thank our lucky stars that we have found solace here together.

We talk until sunset at which time we go outside and watch the darkness come in slowly.

We continue with our silent watch until we fall asleep one by one and venture into our dreams of demolition and death.

We love this demolition and this death. It turns our silent lives into something important. In these dreams we are crushed by concrete and steel or mummified with asbestos. We wake with smiles.

We sit in silence until noon and then pray to our many gods. They are deaf, yes, but they are there. They watch us collapse into the molten river beneath the buildings. The river carries us through the debris and into the open air. We lose consciousness just in time. We love this demolition and death.

We allow our dreams to repeat it.

LX. OFFICIAL REPORT

The doctors are in the basement. They are writing, writing, writing. They are documenting. They are preserving facts.

While they work, they also worry about the mirrors and the twins. They are all still alive and the doctors are surprised by this. They were never meant to survive. The procedure was a dangerous one. Then again, every procedure is dangerous.

Everything is dangerous at all times.

So now the first set of twins have been pulled and the doctors prepare for the next set.

"We shall pull the rest," Dr. Sotos says.

"No one should be expected to provide for such complex organisms," Dr. Corbelli says.

Dr. Visna shakes his head and swallows pills. He says, "We will save the future from itself."

The other doctors laugh and continue to type.

They are preserving facts.

Everything is dangerous at all times.

Dr. Visna gets up, puts in a video tape into the VCR. He presses PLAY. The doctors type while watching the footage.

Grey plumes and ash with skin cells and copier paper, coffee cups, paperclips, staplers and Scotch tape, liquid paper fireworks, fluttering manila folders as death-birds. A blue sky transforming into a face that is beaten with righteous agony. Explosions ripping apart temples and trains.

"We've come to smash mirrors," Dr. Sotos says as he types and watches the television.

"And smother children," Dr. Corbelli says.

Dr. Visna nods and empties the bottle of pills. He looks at the label that says HIDEO PHARMACY. "No refills left," he says. "I will have to do something about that."

"You should see a doctor." Dr. Sotos says.

Dr. Visna giggles.

Dr. Corbelli says, "Shhhhh! I like this part!"

The men look at the television. They watch a building implode. There is no smoke, no dust, no fire. It just implodes into nothing.

"That was a dangerous one!" Dr. Visna says. "Praise the jinn!"

"All of them were dangerous!" Dr. Corbelli adds.

Dr. Sotos claps his hands. "And all of them were fun!"

The doctors laugh.

LXI. RAILROAD STORY

We need a sacrifice.

That's what it is, pure and simple. We go up to the mountain to get our tools. We were told to sacrifice our most prized possessions and that's what we are aiming to do. There is no real choice. There isn't even the illusion of free will. We were told what to do and we will do it.

We need several sacrifices, really. It isn't just one. Again, it isn't like we have a choice. We were told to do it and so we are going to. We received the instructions over the radio and responded right away with agreement. Sure, we'll do it. Of course. We wouldn't have it any other way. We were expecting this. We are welcoming it.

It is the moment we have been waiting for.

With that in mind, you must realize how much of our lives have started to become overshadowed by this sacrifice. Our families and friends have taken a backseat. Our jobs have been lost. Our hobbies have evaporated. We have nothing but our plans.

We have nothing but the sacrifices.

We go up the mountain with our tools. We bring our plans, our blueprints, our sacred documents. We have everything we need.

The Hercules Chemical Plant is located on lower Minisink. It is right by Bailey's Park where that girl's body was found. It is near the DuPont factory.

The Hercules Chemical Plant. Yes, that castle of smokeless powder and chemicals. More than a hundred years old. It has been shut down. No one goes in except for drug addicts and people like us. People like us? Yes, people like us.

We set up shop at the Hercules Plant which has been out of commission for quite a few years. There's a contaminated lake behind it that will work fairly well in our endeavors. We are as prepared as we'll ever be and we are proud.

Before we do anything, we read through our sacred texts and match them up with our blueprints. We take notes. We make recordings. We discuss and debate the content for hours. No, we don't actually accomplish anything but the debates and discussion build morale and make us feel like brothers.

We hear the train in the distance and know that it's time. I tell everyone that all I have to do is go up a few blocks and get my son. Then we'll do what we came to do.

Everyone nods. They bow their heads.

I'm grateful for this show of faith. They believe in me. They trust me. Faith is an important thing, the most important thing. Faith and sacrifice.

That's what life is all about.

LXII. CHOOSING SIDES

Barry opens his eyes and sees the man holding the camera to his face.

"So, you're him?" Barry says. "You're the guy."

The man nods. "I'm the guy."

"I don't blame you, you know."

"Blame me?"

"You know, for sleeping with my wife."

The man shakes his head. "I don't know what to say to that."

"You don't have to say anything. I'm just letting you know that I don't blame you. If I was in your position, I would probably be doing the same thing."

The man nods.

"But why the camera? Why are you filming me?"

"I just like to film things. That's what I do. That's my job."

"Your job? You're a filmmaker?"

The man chuckles. "Not anymore. I'm a researcher."

"Researcher? What do you research?"

"Things."

Barry nods. "Well, are you here to pick up my wife?"

"No."

"What are you here for?"

The man taps the camera. "This."

"Oh. That's it? You want to film me? You want to film the pathetic cuckold?"

"Cuckold?"

"Forget it," Barry says. "So what now?"

"Nothing now," the man says. "I just needed more footage."

"Then get out of my house, now. Okay?"

The man nods. "I will." He walks to the door.

"Aren't you going to say hi to my wife?"

"No. You can do that for me," the man says. "I'm done."

PART TWO:
That Day

I'm reaching for my God like skyscrapers in the night.
-Matisyahu

LXIII. DETRICK MUTTERRECHT

Ronald wishes he hadn't had to drug Susan but that was the only way to get her out of the house short of calling the police and he didn't want to do that. Besides, what would he say? That she's crazy? No, he didn't want to do that.

He puts her into the car and starts driving into the city. It was a drive he used to enjoy but no more. No, now he is full of dread. He thinks about everything his wife has recently talked about and as he drove through the Holland Tunnel, he expects to see a checkpoint set up and populated by a death squad.

He wonders what they'd look like. Would they be white men? Mexicans? Middle-eastern men? Arabs? Jews? Egyptians? Southeastern Asians? Would the death squad be a diverse mix? Would they be heavily armed? Would they have records on everyone, some sort of computerized database? No, Ronald figures it would be a pretty primitive operation at this point. Maybe just clipboards and lots of papers. They would be heavily armed, though, yes. They'd be ready to kill anyone who didn't comply with their orders. Would they strip search him? Would they sodomize him if he didn't follow orders?

Ronald doesn't plan on noncompliance, though. He will obey every command. You have to live by the laws of the land. Rules are rules. Following rules means survival especially in this day and age when there is danger nearly everywhere you go.

He drives through the tunnel but passes no checkpoint, no death squads, no heavily armed guards. He is relieved. He knows he doesn't have the stomach for such confrontation.

Ronald looks at his wife and notices how skinny she has become. She hasn't been eating very well. Ronald is sure that is contributing to her paranoia. A healthy body is a healthy mind, after all.

Ronald drives through the city slowly, slowly, slowly, and is becoming annoyed at the constant stopping despite the fast pace of the environment. He hates the city now. The buildings sandwich him and he hates that, too. He feels pressured. He has the sudden urge to stop the car and get out, leaving Susan to get help on her own. But how would that even work? She'd wake up in the car in the middle of the city. The last thing she'd remember would be taking a sip of orange juice Ronald had poured for her. Her sudden appearance in the city would

surely convince her that everything she has been obsessing about has been correct. She would be convinced of
Ronald's culpability in her predicament. She'd assume
he was part of it. He was a government agent. He was
a member of a death squad, perhaps one specializing in
kidnapping or gang rape. A squad would be waiting to
interrogate her. Or perhaps Ronald was part of some
other covert team, a corporate squad of banker assassins or religious zealots. Anything was possible. Susan
always told him everything was dangerous at all times.

Ronald knows now. Everything is dangerous. Everything and everywhere is dangerous but the city is the
most dangerous place. There are too many buildings,
too many people, too many directions to go, too much
noise, too many bits and pieces. It is a moving map of
chaos with unpredictable machines and unstable structures populated by a volatile and erratic populous. Nothing in the city is as eternal as it appears. The crosswalks
are illusions. There are no safe places for pedestrians.
The lanes on the streets, the cars don't follow the flow,
don't follow the rules of the road because, let's face it,
there are no actual rules. Nothing is set in stone and
even if that was the case, stone is not eternal. Stone can
be chiseled or smashed. Even diligent laws and law enforcement cannot protect people from the hidden fac-
tors that can jump out and pull things out from under.
No day is the same. There are a multitude of new dangers being borne out of every possibility.

Ronald knows his wife too well. If he lets her out

of the car, she would wander terrified. Outwardly she would appear composed but inwardly she would be a petrified pedestrian. She would wander alongside the tallest buildings very slowly as if afraid to wake a sleeping giant for if the giant wakes it might fall over in a drunken stupor. It would take her twenty minutes to pass just one building. She would wonder how the other people could walk by the buildings so fast. They are always so preoccupied with their cell phones and coffee. They never see the danger. They refuse to acknowledge that they are in danger at all times. They laugh off the idea of danger that will eventually annihilate them. They laugh it off. They are oblivious jesters in a wilderness of multiple dangers.

Ronald slows the car down and looks up at the buildings. A ball of terror grows in the pit of his stomach. He does not want to wake the sleeping giants. He does not want them to collapse into drunken tragedy. His car would be crushed. He would be smothered in glass and steel. His life would be ended in this godforsaken city. He'd be nothing but dust.

He stops the car.

LXIV. COLLOIDAL SILVER

Jessica stands looking out the window at the city, the traffic jams, the little people walking to wherever the hell they need to go and she thinks it would be in their best interest if she dropped an explosive device on them.

It is not a morbid or homicidal thought. She is thinking this without hatred or even thoughts of death. Her thoughts are those of non-existence. One second the people would be there and in the next, they would be dust and ash and vapor. She thinks it would be beautiful. It would be like a birth or rebirth or some form of cosmic conception. It would be a transformation of atoms, a newly discovered scientific law, though Jessica knows close to nothing about actual science. She does know that her experiment would cause the people to change, a *natural* change, and she would be the catalyst to that change. There is no hate in her heart or her mind. She is proud to think of herself as a catalyst for that sort of transformation.

She thinks about her rape. Who was the guy again? She doesn't remember his name. No one understood why she would forget the name of the guy who did that but Jessica never understood why she'd be expected to remember it. It wasn't his name that penetrated her, it was the sharp stab of his primal urge. She remembers that his name was something common, though, like Ryan or Nick. She had been smoking weed with him and he made her do things. She was fourteen at the time. He was eighteen.

Jessica thinks about her father. She wonders if her father had ever done anything like that. Had he ever taken drugs? Had he ever forced himself on a girl? She thinks maybe that's why he killed himself. Maybe he had done terrible things like raping women or molesting kids. If she knew for sure that his suicide was a result of guilt, then his death would have meaning and she might be able to forgive him for the suicide if not for the crimes that caused it.

Jessica decides her father was a rapist.

Her father raped fifteen women in the span of thirteen years. He started when he was nineteen years old. His victims were beaten and sodomized. They were made to say vile things while he assaulted them. He recorded their voices saying all of the vile things. He played them back when he was alone so he could masturbate to the abuse.

It is quite possible he was also a victim of government experiments and the urge to rape was a side effect. He simply could not control himself. Finally he could not handle the guilt. He gave himself a death sentence.

Jessica looks out the window and feels an overwhelming feeling of love for the people below her. They will enjoy happiness. They will enjoy every single eternal second of happiness she will bestow upon them. They will experience joy and happiness and paradise. One cannot forget paradise. One has to enjoy it. One has to enjoy happiness.

Enjoy happiness.

LXV. M.I.H.O.P.

My son walks into the kitchen and says, "Your book is a piece of shit."

This surprises me. My son doesn't use that sort of language (at least in front of me) and even though he's outgrown the book I've written, I never thought he had such hatred for it. Of course the only response I have is, "What?"

"Your book is garbage."

"Where is this coming from, Tim?"

"What do you mean, dad? I just wanted to tell you. Your book is shit."

"Okay, just stop using that sort of language. What's gotten into you?"

"Nothing, dad. It's just shit."

"You're out of line," I say. "What you're saying is very hurtful, you know."

"And having to read your stupid book for the last

ten years has been hurtful. Get over it."

My wife walks into the room and says, "Come in quick. Something's happened."

"What?" I say.

"Just come in here." She walks back into the living room. My son and I follow her.

The television is on. Indeed, something has happened. I cannot believe my eyes. It is just like in my book. It's terrifyingly magnificent. It's all I imagined and more.

LXVI. LULLABY SANCTIONS

Tina is crawling across the asphalt. Planes are flying overhead. She is enjoying the sound of engines and voices.
Some of the voices are unusually calm and speaking
ominously about unknown men walking back and forth
to the lavatory, back and forth. Some of the men are
holding fast-food bags. Some are sweating profusely.

Other voices are frantic, rambling expressions of
love expressed in simple and banal terms made no more
important by the sounds of crying accompanying them.

The asphalt turns to wreckage. Tina is crawling
across jagged pieces of steel, glass, fabric, and flesh. She
does not stop crawling. She crawls because she does not
feel blessed enough to walk among the ruins. The ruins
are a work of art, the result of a cosmic surgery. Everything has changed for the better. The ruins are a birth, a
death, a surprise party.

Tina sees her parents in the ruins. Their faces hold

blank expressions of apathy bordering on disapproval. What do they want from her now? Did they want her to lose another part of herself? Did they want her to change even more?

That would be impossible.

Tina is finally herself and she is satisfied being lulled into submission by the airplane sounds above her. She falls asleep smiling.

LXVII. ENJOY HAPPINESS

Jessica dials the number.

"Hello?" a voice answers.

"Timothy?"

"Yeah?"

"My name is Jessica. Someone told me you'd be able to help me."

"Help you with what?"

"Making chocolate."

Silence.

"Hello?" Jessica says.

"I don't know what you're talking about."

"I think you do."

"You have the wrong number."

"Calcutta 1993. Mehola Junction. Hadera. Imam Reza 1994. Capricorn Station 1998. Do those mean anything to you?"

"Why the hell are you calling me?"

"You know why."

"I...I'm not in the business anymore."

"The chocolate business? You're sure?"

"I....Don't call me again."

"Highland Park, last year. Milltown, two months ago."

Silence.

"Do I have your attention?" Jessica says. She is holding the phone with one hand and picking a scab on her nose with the other. She is staring out the window at the city. She sees dozens of planes zigzag across the sky. She hears faint voices.

"You have my attention, yes," Tim says. "But I don't think you're authorized to..."

"I am the bride of the south."

"Okay," the man says. He sighs. "Fine. What exactly do you want?"

"Chocolate."

"Specifically?"

"The purest."

"I'm not into riddles. Get to the point. What's the target?"

"A city."

"Okay, but what specifically?"

"The whole thing."

"Give me a goddamn break."

"I want it all gone."

"Is this a joke? Stop wasting my time."

"If I was able to have dozens of small pieces and

place them in the right areas, it would be possible, right?"

"If you want small pieces, you can do that yourself. There are dozens of recipes on the Internet. This isn't a game."

"I tried. I'm just not good at organizing, preparation…"

"There's not much to it. The small ones, I mean. You tried?"

"Yes but there's just something about it…I can't explain it. I can't do it. I need help."

"We'll have to meet. You'll have to follow my instructions exactly."

"Okay."

"And payment is upfront and nonnegotiable."

"I understand."

"And I need to ask. Where did you get my number?"

"From one of my father's friends."

"Who was your father?"

"People called him the Jumper."

"Oh."

"You remember him."

"Yes, I remember him quite well," Tim says. "We all do."

LXVIII. SABAH FEGHALI

Susan sees a black cloud roll through the city. She screams. Everyone is screaming. Even Ronald is screaming.

How did she get here?

Her head is buzzing. Her mouth is dry. She puts her face against the car window and looks at the sky. Are those planes? Of course they are. Was she expecting anything other than airplanes? They are everywhere.

Death squads.

They are taking to the air now. They are riding in on black clouds of dust and chunky ash. There is no escape. The death squads are engulfing cars and pedestrians.

She hears explosions from several directions.

They are everywhere. She turns to Ronald. He is bleeding and screaming. He is not going to save her. Susan knows this.

The black cloud moves in and takes over the car.

Loud music starts to play. At first Susan thinks it's coming from the car radio but then realizes it's coming from outside. It's coming from speakers on top of the skyscrapers.

It is a sound that rattles the car and tickles Susan's eardrums. She can no longer see outside the windows but she can hear the music just fine. It is a hypnotic din, a call to some sort of terrifying prayer.

Susan opens the glove compartment and starts pulling things out. Lipstick, tire gauge, insurance card, car manual, breath mints, a pen, loose cigarettes, receipts, safety pins, dust.

Ronald stops screaming to say, "What are you looking for?"

Susan says nothing. She doesn't know what she's looking for.

LXIX. SAMIRA SAID

"I'm running a goddamn business, not a charity."

"That's not what people think."

"I don't care what people think."

"Well, you should start. Things are getting intense."

"So?"

"Dangerous, too. I don't even want to go over to the offices anymore. You should see what's happening over there."

"Don't be so negative. We'll get this done and that's that."

"And what about the films? I don't have the master copies and I haven't heard from our guy yet."

"He'll call."

"You sure?"

"I said he'll call. Why do you doubt me so much?"

"I'm not doubting *you*. I'm doubting *him*."

"Okay, but I hired him and if you are casting any

doubt on his reliability, I take offense to that. We'll have the videos. We'll have the cassettes. We'll have the booklets. We'll have everything in time."

"Okay. I still think we need to write Henwich a check."

"I told you, we're a business."

"It'll be a show of good faith."

"I don't believe in faith."

"That's funny."

"Is it?"

"Ironic, I mean."

"How about you go deal with the buildings and stop bothering me?"

"It's all taken care of."

"There's a lot more that needs to get done."

"It's being taken care of right now."

"Then just leave."

"You got it."

"Oh, one more thing…"

"Yeah?"

"Shut that goddamn radio off."

LXX. BHUTTO BHUTTO BHUTTO

TIMOTHY OSMAN SPEARS was contacted at his home. After being advised of the identity of the interviewing agent and the fact that he was being interviewed regarding the possible presence of suspected terrorist SALEM BAYLEY AL-HENWICH aboard American Airlines AA flight number 23 on May 29, 2001, Mr. SPEARS provided the following information:

Four weeks ago I received a call from our recruitment office in Manhattan. Someone had sent an anonymous package which contained five-hundred photocopied pages of a document we had thought was lost to history. Not only did we think it was lost but we *wanted* it lost, if you know what I mean.

Someone had gone to the trouble of copying all of those pages and sending it to our recruitment office, knowing full well that word would get to me and that I would take the first flight to NYC in order to figure out the situation. At the time, I didn't really know who that someone was but in hindsight, there shouldn't even have been a question. There should have never been a mystery. I should have known all along and I blame myself for that, really.

So when the recruitment office received the package, they contacted me and I took the next flight to NYC despite my extreme fear of flying. Previously I had only traveled to the east coast via train, car, or bus. However, this incident in question was something that needed to be taken care immediately and so I boarded a plane with a head full of anti-anxiety medication. Flying is an unnatural act and I despise it. It's dangerous, you know. It's the most dangerous thing in the world, I think.

When I reached NYC, I was a foggy mess. That was okay, though. With the help of some prescription head-clearers, I got focused and took a cab to the recruitment office. When I got there, all I saw was the swirling lights of law enforcement. That was not a good sign.

Then I saw the ambulances and the fire trucks.

The recruitment center (consisting of five floors in a 25 story building) was no more. Someone had piloted a small passenger plane into the fourth and fifth floors. The place was on fire. The back part of the plane (I don't know the technical term) was sticking out and I remember that it reminded me of the tail of a shrimp.

In the crowd gathering outside the building, I spotted Peter. The cab let me out and I slowly slid beside him. I asked him what happened and he told me that one of our employees had the package and that he had run off with it. That's when I saw a man on a bicycle. I initially told the authorities that the man resembled a giraffe, a giraffe on a bicycle.

I did think that was strange and it crossed my mind that perhaps I had been drugged without my knowledge. In my business, it is not uncommon for people to slip substances into the food or drinks of unsuspecting colleagues.

The next thing I remember is being on the flight home. I do remember asking the flight attendant (Ms. JIMENEZ) if I could tour the cockpit. I admit this is out of character for me and that is precisely the reason why I suspect I was drugged. A man walked up behind me (Mr. AL-HENWICH) and also requested a tour of the cockpit. I did not know that man but I later found out he had been seated next to me on both the flight to and from NYC. He had the aisle seat and I was in the middle. I must have had to walk over him several times to use the lavatory but I hadn't remembered him.

What he ended up doing, I had no previous knowledge of. During my first interview, it was brought up that I had borrowed the man's laptop on the flight *to* NYC but I have no recollection of that. They showed me the laptop, showed me files that proved I had logged into several programs (programs I had never heard of) and I basically gave up at that point. I must have been drugged and must have been unable to control my actions. I tried explaining the business I'm in and how these things do happen but my interviewers would not accept my explanations. I asked to make a phone call. They granted me that. They gave me one phone call and I called the only person who I thought would understand my predicament.

LXXI. FINALLY, ROTATION

Ronald and Susan snuggle in the backseat.

People are outside banging on the car. They aren't visible because the grey dust has caked the windows.

Ronald says, "What's happening?"

"You know what's happening," Susan says.

"No, I don't believe it. I can't believe it."

"You trust me, don't you, Ron? I'm your wife and you trust me, right?"

"Yes, yes, I trust you, Susan."

"Then why don't you believe me? You know who they are."

"No!"

"You know, Ron."

The poundings on the door get louder. Someone sends a fire axe through the window. Glass goes everywhere.

Susan screams. "Death squads!"

LXXII. A MORE MEANINGFUL ANNIHILATION

Jessica walks slowly through the city.

Things are going as planned. She has a first class seat to reconciliation. She is no longer the rape victim. She is no longer the daughter of a suicide. She is no longer the offspring of a rapist. She is no longer herself. She is *post*-Jessica.

She hears the sounds reverberate block after block. Explosions, first, and then screams. She smiles. Things are working out for the best. She will never be raped again. She will never be disappointed again. Many more daughters will lose their fathers to the urban curse of tall buildings and the temptation to jump. There will be men just like her father who will choose their own method of death. Yes, there will be more jumpers.

Jessica finally turns around and sits on the curb. She sees a gigantic grey-brown cloud of dust engulf the street, coming closer and closer. She extends her arms for her father.

She is not sad anymore.

LXXIII. AQEDAH

"Honey?"

"Barry?"

"No, it's Tim."

"What are you talking about?"

"It's Tim. I might be in trouble."

"What's going on? Why are you talking like this, Barry?""

"Three Middle Eastern men walk into a bar. The first man orders a cola and the bartender gives him a look of pity and then the second man orders a light beer and the bartender gives him a look of, uh, shame. Then the third man orders nothing but instead he whispers something into the bartender's ear."

"Barry, what the hell is wrong with you?"

"This is Tim, honeybunch."

"Jesus Christ…"

"You know my father wrote me a letter."

"Barry…"

"He confessed that he was going to name me Isaac."

"Barry…"

"That would have been ironic, don't you think?"

"Jesus, Barry!"

"Jesus doesn't walk into the bar. Not in *this* joke, anyway. There is an explosion and the firemen show up. They're pretty traumatized at what they see, you know, like bodies all burned and stuff. Some of the bodies look like they've been cannibalized or something. They don't really know. How could you expect them to? They aren't trained for that sort of thing. But the joke about Jesus, I don't remember how the whole thing goes. Maybe something like Jesus Christ walks into the bar and walks up to the bartender who happens to be a djinn and the djinn offers him three wishes. First Jesus asks for the ability to raise the dead. Then he asks for the ability to turn water into wine. Then he asks for the ability to fly. The djinn laughs and grants him all those wishes and then BOOM, the whole bar explodes and everyone dies."

"Barry, I'm hanging up!"

"Honey, wait!"

"What?"

"Do you smell that?"

"What?"

"It smells like jet fuel."

LXXIV. TABORICA COMMAND CENTER

The three doctors are popping pills.

They are now on the 23rd floor of the *other* building. They have a VCR set up and are watching XNOY-BIS SUPER TERRORIST FORCE SIX in its original Japanese with no English subtitles. None of the doctors speak Japanese but they understand what's going on in the movie nonetheless.

They understand everything that is going on inside the room as well as outside of the building.

They know and understand what is happening in the streets as they sit in the room, swallowing pills and watching as skyscrapers attack civilians on the television. They understand the screams and the sirens.

The three doctors are popping pills. They will do so until they no longer understand what is happening. They will do so until they no longer hear the screams or the sirens or the Japanese dialogue.

They will do so until they no longer understand their sickness.

Amen.

LXXV. WHAT WE KNOW

"This is captain."

"Sit down!"

"No more! No more!"

"Shut up! I cut your throat!"

"I have kids! Please! Please!"

"Praise him! I cut your throat!"

"No!"

"Everything is fine. I finished."

"They want to get in here!"

"Shut the door!"

"No! No!"

"Tell him I love him."

"He is the greatest! We pull it down! We pull it down!"

"Ladies and gentlemen, here the captain, I am and please remain seating. We, they have bomb on board plane so sit and we will land and get our demands. This is captain."

"I don't want to die!"

"Our father who art in…"

"I cut your throat!"

"Tell the kids I love them."

"I don't want to die!"

"Pull it."

"Do the orders still stand?"

"Of course!"

"I love you."

"I cut your throat!"

"I have kids!"

"Roll it. Cut off the oxygen."

"…is the greatest!"

"Father!"

"They want to get in here. Hold, hold from the inside."

"Tell them I love them."

"Is that it? I mean, shall we pull it down?"

"Two passengers have had their throats cut."

"Everything is fine. I finished."

"…is the greatest!"

"I cut your throat!"

"…is the greatest!"

"Father who…"

"I cut your…"

"Father…"

"Tell the kids I love them."

"Down, down, down. Sit down. Shut up."

"Oh God!"

"…is the greatest!"

"I bear witness that there is no other…"

"Let's go."

"Stay back!"

"How gracious!"

"Let's get them!"

"When they all come, we finish it off."

"Everything is fine. I finished."

"God is the greatest!"

"I cut your throat."

"Tell my kids I love them."

LXXVI. GREEN TEA AND MACA

Barry is on the street now.

He sees the event as it happens and is glad he does not have to wait to see it on the television. Nothing he has ever experienced before has been this intense. He cannot help but feel invigorated. His batteries are charged.

He is not being idle, however.

There are people on the ground, people screaming for help. There are dead bodies, too, bodies that resemble the citizens of Pompeii.

Barry grabs a man's hand and pulls him up. He brushes dust out of the man's eyes. A woman grabs Barry's ankle. He helps her up as well. He touches her face.

Screams and sirens come up from all sides. Barry winces. Everything is too loud. Something hits him in the head and he feels gritty blood run down his face. Barry continues to pull people up off the ground and as he is helping people, he feels his penis become erect.

Soon he is assisting people indiscriminatingly, pushing or pulling them out of the way of debris while his arousal reaches a fever pitch. He yearns for his wife. He yearns for one more chance at intercourse with her. But he knows she would not want him in this condition. He is simply *not himself.*

On a sidewalk across the street there is the man with the camera again. He is filming Barry. Next to him stands a Japanese man who Barry recognizes. The man is holding a handheld tape recorder. He is recording the sounds of the event. He hopes to make copies of the recording and sell them in his shop.

Barry waves to the men but they don't acknowledge him.

Papers fall in front of his face. Something else hits him in the head. His ears clog with dust. His heart is pounding fast and hard, causing his erection to throb as he tries to pull a man out of a taxi.

There is a loud roar. Barry looks up to the sky and through the veil of dust he sees a plane flying low and very slowly. It appears to slow down, goes slower and slower towards the direction of the huge grey cloud that is approaching Barry from the west.

He ejaculates but it is a joyless orgasm. It is simply a release. His body has decided to rid Barry of desire. He stops helping the people around him and has a seat on the curb. He leans back and lets the dust fall over him like a slow shower. He lets the papers, pens, and pencils hit him. He bathes in the shards of wooden desks and the innards of destroyed computers. Barry lets out a sigh of relief.

He stands up from the curb and runs into the dust cloud.

LXXVII. MY CITY, MY TOMB

There is no solace now, no quarter, no safe haven. There is only the *descent*.

The ceiling is falling. The floor is falling. The walls float between them. They float with us. There is a freefall along with the deafening roar that is both gentle and terrifying. I cannot hear you but I see your face. You have the look of an infant frightened by the unknown. I am sure I share the same expression.

My bladder weakens but I am not concerned. It is warm and it feels nice.

I am falling with you and you with me and all the rest of the people who were mostly strangers but now are partners in our descent.

It takes us ten seconds to reach the bottom but it feels like several lifetimes pass and we use the time to wonder whether we should care about where we end up after all of this is over.

We will be mixed with concrete dust and molten steel. We will be cremated against our wishes. This building will encase us in a demolished mausoleum.

Nothing matters in this moment, not my impotence, not my back pain, not my anxiety about leaving the house, not the lump in my testicles, not the stress I have over my job, not my feelings of disappointment.

But I'm not sad.

I feel as if things will finally be settled. All the fear and anxiety I have felt were leading up to something, leading up to this: my descent into a metropolitan grave, a grave we will share.

There is no solace now, no quarter, no safe haven.

But I'm not sad. I have no regrets but one. I wish I had taken my son fishing.

I hope he will forgive me.

COPELAND
VALLEY

www.ingramcontent.com/pod-product-compliance
Lightning Source LLC
Chambersburg PA
CBHW020405150626
46554CB00012B/273